PRAISE FOR
THE GIRL ON THE BOAT

"The word adventure is often overused. We attach it to all sorts of activities where the outcome is assured ahead of time. A roller coaster, for instance, is not an adventure. We know what will happen, where it will go, and where it will end. An adventure, by definition, has to be an activity where we're not quite sure what will happen, where it will take us, or how it will end. The Girl on the Boat *lays the perfect foundation for a true rollicking adventure. Once you step on board with Bailey, Monica, and Captain Tommy, you'll never guess where you're headed."*

~ David Congdon, Threat Assessment and
Countermeasures Specialist

"Danielle has done it again. I find myself looking forward to her next book in the Mailboat series before I've even finished reading the latest one."

~ Sam Petitto, police consultant and competitive writer

Danielle Lincoln Hanna

THE GIRL
ON THE BOAT

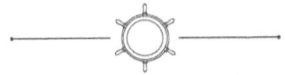

HHP

HEARTH & HOMICIDE PRESS, LLC
MISSOULA, MT
2020

Paperback: ISBN 978-1-7330813-7-5
eBook: ISBN 978-1-7330813-8-2

BOOKS BY DANIELLE LINCOLN HANNA

The Mailboat Suspense Series

The Girl on the Boat: A prequel novella to the Mailboat
Suspense Series
Mailboat I: The End of the Pier
Mailboat II: The Silver Helm
Mailboat III: The Captain's Tale
Mailboat IV - *coming summer 2020*

DanielleLincolnHanna.com/shopnow

JOIN THE CREW

Ahoy, Shipmate!

If you feel like you're perched on a lighthouse, scanning the horizon for Danielle Lincoln Hanna's next book—good news! You can subscribe to her email newsletter and read a regular ship's log of her writing progress. Better yet, dive deep into the life of the author, hear the scuttlebutt from her personal adventures, spy on her writing process, and catch a rare glimpse of dangerous sea monsters—better known as her pets, Fergus the cat and Angel the German Shepherd.

It's like a message in a bottle washed ashore. All you have to do is open it...

DanielleLincolnHanna.com/newsletter

THE GIRL
ON THE BOAT

MONDAY
JUNE 10, 2013

CHAPTER ONE
STEPH

Not even a dog barked tonight. Not a single call for service. Not so much as a car found in a no-parking zone. Telecommunicator Steph Buchanan leaned on her hand at her desk in the Communications Center and sipped more coffee, staring at the two dots on her screen that represented the two officers patrolling Lake Geneva. They'd been driving circles since their shift began, looking for something to do. It had been an hour since anyone touched the radio.

A light flickered below her monitors and her eyes dropped to the bank of illuminated switches. Peeling labels designated *lobby door, hall door,* etc. They glowed a light yellow-green, signaling she could flip the switch and unlock a door.

One had turned red. *Garage.*

There were only two ways to open any of the doors in the station. Steph could trigger them from her workstation. Or an officer could cue the door with the key cards they carried in their pockets. Around here, the butt-swipe dance was well-known. Cops walked rear-end-first into doors so the sensors at hip-height could scan their cards.

There was just one problem. There were only two officers on duty tonight. And Steph knew from the map on her monitor they were nowhere near the station.

She frowned at the red switch as it flashed back to yellow-green. Maybe one of the detectives or the lieutenant had come in. But two in the morning? That was odd. She looked up at the feeds from the security cameras, turning her eye to the one posted in the garage. Black and white SUVs sat in silent rows, facing the center aisle for fast deployment. Patrol bikes, used in the crowded tourist district near the lakefront, lined one wall, parked next to a pair of motorcycles.

At the far end of the garage, a door swung shut. Steph was just in time to see a leg and foot vanish through it and noted another switch turn red on her dashboard.

There was nothing through that door but locker rooms, the gym, evidence intake, and storage rooms. They didn't have security cameras in those rooms. No one but officers ever went there.

Steph's radio mic sat in a little stand on her desk. She pushed the button. "Forty-four o-six and forty-four ten, report your status."

Static crackled. "Forty-four o-six. I saw a black cat just now," Officer Dan Norton drolled.

"Forty-four ten. I saw it fifteen minutes ago in front of the bakery," Officer Shelby Serrano replied. "It looked highly suspicious. At next sighting, we should pull it over for questioning."

"Copy that," said Norton.

Steph rolled her eyes. She didn't feel like cop humor right now. "I'm just checking your GPS is working. Neither of you returned to the station, right?"

"Negative," they each reported in turn.

"Okay. Somebody walked in. Probably just the lieutenant. I think he said he'd be in early—I just didn't think this early. I'm taking five to check it out."

"Need backup?" Serrano asked.

It reminded Steph of her college days, walking across campus after dark. *Give me a minute,* another female classmate from your dorm would say. *I'll walk with you.* But Serrano's offer of camaraderie existed on a different plane; no one wanted to mess with the sisterhood of bad-ass butt-kickers that were female cops.

"Negative," Steph said. "I'm sure it's fine." It was far-fetched to think anyone could have entered the station besides an officer.

"Copy," Serrano said. "Radio if you change your mind."

"Ten-four." Steph stood up from her station and grabbed a portable radio. She turned the volume low; she wasn't sure why. Out in the hall, she opted against the elevator and took the stairs. They were quieter. On the lower level, she used her own key card and quietly pushed open the door to the patrol car bay. Automatic lights flickered alive, cold and white. The patrol units stared at her through blind headlights, silent, and yet she almost expected them to breathe, sigh, berate her for interrupting their slumber. She tip-toed across the garage to the far door, hip-checked the key card sensor, and pushed the door open. The hall beyond was dimly lit by recessed lights. She waited for her eyes to adjust, then crept forward.

Half the doors in this hallway, even Steph couldn't open. Only the men, for instance, had the combination to the men's locker room door; only the chief, the lieutenant, and the detectives had keys to the evidence and records storage rooms. One set of doors, Steph didn't care for much, the ones labeled MAINTENANCE. Something about changing air pressure from the heating unit caused those doors to rattle exactly when you weren't expecting. The veterans loved telling the newbies the doors were haunted.

Steph crept past them—quiet tonight—and around a bunch of two-by-fours leaning against the wall, God only knew why they were there. Maybe someone had planned to build more shelving in the storage rooms once upon a time.

She checked the knob to the evidence storage room. Tightly locked, as it should be. She peered to the door at the end of the hall. The records room was lined with boxes of paper files, row upon row of them, relics from the days before the Lake Geneva Police Department had standardized electronic systems.

The door was cracked open. This one was secured with a good, old-fashioned metal key. Either the lieutenant had entered with his key or the lock had been forced. A light bobbed inside as if it came from a phone or a flashlight.

"Hello?" she called before thinking it through. The lieutenant would have turned on the overhead lights.

The flash vanished. The room at the end of the hall went pitch black.

Steph lifted her radio to her lips, hand trembling, and said something she'd never said before. "LGPD, requesting backup."

The radio crackled quietly and Shelby Serrano's voice came over the air. "Ten four. ETA, ten minutes."

Steph let her hand drop to her side and watched the door like a hawk. She was a dispatcher. A telephone cop. She'd walked people through countless emergencies, but she'd always had the safety of a phone line between her and whatever was happening. Sometimes her butt clenched at what she heard on the other end of the line, her jaw screwed tight at her inability to do more than advise and wait. But she didn't have half the equipment the patrol officers did. She didn't have a gun. She didn't have handcuffs. She didn't so much as have a flashlight. All she had—all she ever had—was her radio.

A rattling bang split the air as dramatically as a gunshot. Steph's heart leapt into her throat and she whirled. The haunted doors. They rattled aggressively, fighting against their own latch as if skeletal hands demanded release.

Something hard struck the back of her head. Stars burst before her eyes. Then there was blackness and a sense that the floor was coming up to meet her.

CHAPTER TWO
BAILEY

The Mailboat towered over me, all two decks painted navy and white. Lake water splashed along the hull and churned against the pier posts. My heart pounded. Jumping off and getting the mail in the box was the easy part, everybody knew that. But getting back on board? Good luck.

The boat never stopped.

If you didn't gather your courage in time, you could end up standing on the pier like a piece of deck furniture. You might find yourself stupidly watching the windows flash by, filled with the faces of tourists eager to see the show or the splashdown. There was nothing to focus on. Where did you put your hands? Where did you put your feet? Not to mention that gaping maw that was three feet of roiling water between the boat and the pier.

But once the mail was in the box, you just had to go for it.

I'd never done this before.

All these terrors flashed through my mind in the time it took a cricket to breathe. I inhaled deeply and clenched my fists. Bounced on my heels. I could do this. I could do this! I took a step back, winding up for the spring, then pounded across the decking and flung myself over the watery gap between the pier and the boat.

Time slowed. Sunlight glinted off hungry, chomping waves, waiting for me to miss, to slip, to plummet into the ravished belly of the lake.

My fingers found the handrail, cold metal pressing into the grooves of my palms. My sneakers hit the rub board and its gritty, slip-proof surface. My body crashed into a window with a rattle of its metal casing. I'd made it. I'd made it! I paused half a second to soak in the shock and the glory of it all. As the Mailboat rocked gently in the water, me sticking to its side, relief washed down my spine. Maybe I could do this after all. Maybe I could be a for-real Lake Geneva mail jumper. A smile as wide as the lake spread across my face.

"You're doing it wrong," said a voice behind me.

I started and turned, facing a pier which the boat had never left behind—never left behind because it wasn't going anywhere—wasn't going anywhere because this wasn't a tour. And I wasn't a mail jumper.

But Baron Hackett was, the boy who'd coolly informed me I was screwing up my own dearest dream. He stood there, tanned as a sailor, arms like masts, a glittering diamond in his ear and all. His neck was almost too thick for the knotted leather strap he wore around it, a creamy cowrie shell fastened to the center. He was everything a mail jumper should be: cool, calm, athletic.

And me? I was the concessions girl. Right now, I was supposed to be stocking the Mailboat's snack bar for a private charter. Instead, my handcart sat on the pier, the frost on the sides of a dozen ice cream cartons slowly melting and running down.

On the shore beyond the pier, the Riviera Ballroom sat like a squatty old fortress, its arched and pillared windows blinking sleepily at the unfolding drama, just one of a million it must have witnessed over the past eighty years.

It had already seen all the action. This was where the jazz bands used to come up from Chicago and the flapper girls used to swing the night away. Tied up all around me were the other boats of the cruise line fleet, steam launches and stern-wheeled paddle boats old enough to remember the Charleston and the Cakewalk before that and even the Virginia Reel. I doubted any of them cared that I wanted to shrivel up inside a clam shell right now and sink to the bottom of the lake.

Baron combed spiky black bangs out of his eyes, deep and mysterious as underwater caverns but glinting with humor like treasure you didn't expect to find. Maybe he thought my efforts at mail jumping were laughable. "You trying out tomorrow?" he asked.

I slid off the rub board onto the pier and backed up against a pier post. "Tryouts?" I rubbed my arm nervously. "Um... maybe?" At the start of every summer, the kids who worked at the cruise line had a chance to compete for a place on the elite mail jumping team.

Baron motioned toward the boat. "You'll hurt yourself doing it like that."

I didn't get it. "Huh?"

God, this conversation was weird on so many levels— besides me being an idiot. Baron didn't talk to people. He was way too cool for that. He was the quarterback on our high school football team at just sixteen, a year older than me. He was in the National Honor Society. His family owned a mansion on the lake—one of the newer ones on the South Shore that probably had an AI for a butler. "Jeeves, turn on the lights." You know, like that. His sister had been a teen star in a hit TV series. I'm not even kidding. Her first month at school, she brought her own security guard, until her family figured out this was Wisconsin and the crowning of Miss Cheese Days at the nearby Green County Cheese Fest was still a big deal.

And did I mention Baron was a mail jumper? Around here, that was bigger than homecoming king.

"Never run straight at the boat," he explained. "You gotta run at an angle. Because of momentum, you know?" He hovered a palm mid-air and pushed it forward like a little ship through the waves. "The boat's moving this way, right?"

I nodded. "Okay."

The first two fingers of Baron's other hand became a tiny person, running toward the pretend boat. "If you run straight at the boat and grab on, you'll swing backwards like a door on a hinge and slam into the side." The finger person rotated and banged into his thumb. I remembered how I'd smashed into the windows, even with the boat sitting still. "You'll be black and blue all over. Right? So you have to get your momentum going *with* the boat." The finger person tried again, this time running parallel to the boat a few steps before jumping on. "Run at an angle, see?"

I nodded and rubbed my arm some more, trying to massage away my nerves. Now that he explained it, I felt like an idiot. Did good mail jumping candidates automatically know this stuff? Maybe I wasn't cut out to be a mail jumper.

And yet it was all I wanted in the world.

A hearty laugh rang out from the next pier over. Already dying of embarrassment, I was relieved for an excuse to turn my eyes away from Baron. On the other pier, talking with our boss, stood a man in a white shirt with gold and blue stripes on the shoulders. Tommy Thomlin. His uniform was navy-smart, the creases in his sleeves and shorts no doubt measured with a ruler. But just as predictably as his strict attention to detail was the smile on his face as he laughed at something our boss had said, or just as likely, something he had said himself.

He'd been captain of the Mailboat almost fifty years, as reliable as the mail itself. It blew my mind. I'd lived in foster care since I was five, and in my world, people dumped you for any reason. Maybe I colored on the wall; wouldn't eat my veggies; came down with the flu and threw up in the car. I wasn't their child. They weren't obligated to keep me. A simple phone call magically made me somebody else's problem. My own parents had opted to let me be somebody else's problem. And now my mom was dead and my dad just a nameless, faceless, non-figure in my life.

I wasn't sure why, but I lived for those few tours I got to ride the Mailboat with Captain Tommy, sitting behind the snack bar with my chin in my palm and listening to his steady voice like a calming rain. I'd never had a real dad or a grandpa or even an uncle—but if I had, I'd want him to be like Tommy. All last summer, I'd dreamed of the day I would finally be eligible to try out for mail jumping.

And now that day was almost here and I didn't know sticks.

"So, are you going to be here tomorrow morning?" Baron asked. His voice jerked me back to reality like a hand reaching into the lake, pulling me to the surface. I'd basically forgotten I was in the middle of a conversation with anyone.

I looked up at his brawny form, his bright yet strangely veiled eyes. Maybe I wasn't tough enough to be a mail jumper. Maybe you needed to be strong and smart and popular like Baron. Maybe you needed to *be somebody*— and all my life I'd been a nobody, invisible to everyone, and frankly, I liked it better that way.

But still, I'd spent a whole summer selling peanuts just so I could try out as a mail jumper. So... was I going to be here?

I scrunched my sleeve in my fist and bit my lip. "I guess?"

Baron laughed and shook his head, his eyes dipping down. I noticed he had long, dark lashes—but that kind of

11

detail only mattered to fashion models and Olympians, the kind of girls who were actually eligible to talk to Baron Hackett. The kind of girls who mattered.

"Well, I think you should try out," he said, his lashes sweeping up again in the way girls-who-mattered would notice. "Any kid who practices dry runs on the dock clearly wants to be a mail jumper."

What a funny idea. I should be a mail jumper because I wanted to be? I was the bobber on somebody else's fishing line—pulled this way and that by fish and by angler. When had I ever been allowed to want anything? But maybe that was the difference between Baron and me. He was allowed to want things, and then he just went and did them. Maybe that was how he was always in the school newspaper while I vended snacks.

Baron lifted his backpack from the pier to his shoulder. "Well, hope to see you tomorrow."

He turned to go. As he did, something small and white fluttered down from an open pocket on his backpack. As it flipped and flopped, I caught glimpses of a magnetic strip on one side. The card sailed towards the cracks in the pier.

"Hey!" I shouted more to the card than to Baron. I pounced forward and clapped both hands over it. Relief washed over me as I felt the plastic pressed firmly between my palms and the wooden boards.

What a silly credit card, trying to get away like that. It would have spent the rest of its life at the bottom of the lake, and what good would that have done it? Peeling back my hands, I looked at the plastic escapee, expecting to see either the magnetic strip or the string of numbers.

Instead, I saw the emblem of a sailboat inside a circle—the same image on the city's flag. Printed around the circle were the words CITY OF LAKE GENEVA POLICE DEPARTMENT. I flipped it over and looked at the magnetic strip again. What was this thing? It looked like the key cards they give you in hotels...

Baron's lips were parted in a little *O* and his thin black eyebrows arched, the way you would look if you were both surprised and embarrassed, as if the injured baby bunny you were hiding in your backpack had hopped out in the middle of chemistry class. (Not that I speak from experience.)

"Oh wow," he said, "thanks for catching that." He thrust his hand out.

"What is it?" I asked, standing, staring at the card still in my hands. What did it mean, police department...?

"It's nothing," Baron said. He snapped it out of my fingers and shoved it into his back pocket. "Uh... my dad uses a meeting room at City Hall."

Oh, well that made sense, I guess. City Hall and the police station were in the same building. And Baron's dad was the kind of guy who knew every politician, every financial big-wig, all the important people. I could see him needing to meet with the local lawmakers often enough to have his own key card to City Hall.

But then why did Baron have the card? And why did it say "Police Department" and not "City Hall"?

"Gotta run," Baron said. "See you tomorrow." He waved and made long strides down the pier.

I watched him jog away, my head still swimming with questions. Then I stared at the boat. It had suddenly transformed into a bargeful of intimidation. What was I doing, hoping to be a mail jumper? What was I doing, wanting anything at all? I didn't even notice Tommy walk down the pier and stand next to me.

"I think it's soft enough to scoop now," he said.

I jerked my head around. "Huh?"

He grinned and nodded at my hand cart. The cardboard ice cream tubs were going slouchy. I let out a little wail and dashed to pull off a lid. The pecan praline was swimming in pools of its own melted goo. My heart sank. A good mail jumper needed to be sharp—and I couldn't even keep ice cream frozen. Would this be counted against me tomorrow?

Tommy chuckled. "If you hurry, I think it's salvageable." He nodded to the aft deck of the Mailboat. "Go put it in the freezer."

I crammed the lid back on and hurried to shove the hand cart up the ramp. On board the small, enclosed rear deck, I knelt on the floor behind the snack bar, flung open the little freezer, and began unloading ice cream. From the corner of my eye, I saw Tommy arranging tables and chairs on the main deck, a short flight of stairs below me.

A ring tone jingled. Tommy took his cell phone out of the holder on his belt, looked at the screen, and picked up the call. "Well, good morning, sir," he said cheerfully. "What can I do for you?"

There was silence as the other person talked. I knocked a chunk of ice off the side of the freezer so I could fit one more tub of ice cream.

"Last night?" Tommy said, as if repeating the caller's words. The tone of his voice had changed. All of a sudden, it was really heavy and serious, like a stone dropped into the lake. I peeked around the counter. Tommy had stopped arranging chairs and stood in the middle of the deck. He listened a while longer, a hand on his belt, then pulled a chair out from a table and sat down. "Is she okay?"

This sounded serious, whatever it was. Maybe a friend was sick? A family member?

Tommy shook his head at whatever his friend was saying. "No, I haven't heard the kids say anything. But I'll keep my ears open." He waved his fingers slightly, as if brushing a thought away. "Oh, don't mention it." As his friend continued to speak, Tommy's brow went heavy. His lips parted slightly, but his jaw went tight, as if he were ready to bite something off. I held my breath. It took something serious to get him mad, yet me and the other kids knew better than to cross him. He ran this boat like it was the Navy. "Wade, don't be ridiculous. None of these kids would break into a police station, much less attack a dispatcher."

Attack a dispatcher? Wow, that was pretty serious.

Wait...

Ice shot through my veins, and I was pretty sure it had nothing to do with the ice cream. I ducked back behind the snack bar and leaned against the shelves, my heart beating fast.

Baron...?

No, what was I thinking? This was Baron Hackett we were talking about. He was the golden boy. The top student in his class—in the entire school. The future President of the United States, for gosh sake. He wouldn't.

But he had a key card. And it said *Police Department,* not *City Hall...*

CHAPTER THREE
MONICA

"Have you ever seen the person in this photo?"

The homeowner sighed like he'd love nothing more than for me to clear off his porch so he could get to work. I drummed my fingers on the detective's badge clipped to my belt, equally impatient, and didn't so much as shuffle my feet apologetically. Well, screw him. It wasn't *his* co-worker who'd been smacked on the skull with a two-by-four and sent to the ER with a concussion. We were family at the PD, a tight-knit pack—though I was less the nurturing mother wolf and more the crazed hellhound bent on retribution. *Don't piss off Monica Steele* was practically the first thing they taught the rookies, and the last thing I'd ever taught my asshole of an ex.

The man set down his briefcase then snatched the photo out of my hand and screwed up his eyes. "You're kidding, right?" he said, snapping the print-out with his fingernail. "This is the back of his head."

Gee, really? I could also have pointed out that the individual from the security camera footage had pulled up the hood of their sweatshirt, obscuring even their hair cut and color, and had never turned their eyes up higher than the floor. I didn't so much as know whether it was a man or a woman. "It's the best we have," I said, my lips moving naturally—smiling, even—but my molars grinding together.

This was a joke and I knew it, knocking door-to-door with that stupid excuse of a mugshot. But this was me we were talking about. If I had so much as a scrap of a clue, I'd lock my jaws on it like a tenacious dog.

"Did you see anything suspicious last night?"

The man shook his head. "All quiet."

It was the same story on every street—the few streets we had the luxury of getting stories from. The Lake Geneva Police Station was located in the middle of a lot of businesses and parking lots. The building with the best view of our back door—the door that had been accessed by the perpetrator—was the Geneva Lake Museum, a long, low, red brick building across the street. But no one staffed that building until ten a.m., unless you counted the plush Dalmatian that sat on the front seat of a nineteen-teens fire engine.

With so few doors to turn to, my partner and I had broadened our search to include the nearest residential streets, a few blocks away. But so far from the station, I may as well show my crappy photo to the cracks in the sidewalk.

I tucked the picture back into my black leather portfolio, snapped it shut, and nodded at the homeowner. "Thanks for your time. If you think of anything, just give us a call." I handed him a business card. We said a brief good-bye and he grabbed up his briefcase before I was even off his porch.

I strode down the sidewalk back to the PD, cursing my luck. Our station was bristling with security cameras inside and out, yet all we had was the shadowy image of a tall, thin person in black sweat pants and a black hoodie. Steph had never seen him or her at all. The fact that someone had successfully snuck under our radar boiled my blood. And the big question: What had they wanted?

Back at the station, my partner, Detective Sergeant Stan Lehman, leaned against the pale brickwork near the employee entrance, enjoying the shade of a nearby tree.

"Great morning for a stroll, eh?" he said, twirling a pocket-sized spiral-bound notebook between his finger and thumb. After each spin, he tapped the notebook on his thigh, sliding his fingers to the opposite end. Started over. The pages of his notebook must be as empty as mine.

Like me, he wore tan dress pants and a black polo shirt, a badge embroidered on the left breast, his actual badge and service weapon carried on his belt. Unlike me, the beginning of a midlife midriff pulled at his belt and his hair grew in spiky silver blades. You'd never know we were close in age, forty-something. But the women of my family were blessed with dark locks for life—my grandma had died with a full head of mahogany hair at the age of ninety. I pulled mine into a ponytail every morning and ran five miles along the lake shore. Years of the routine had left me ready to run to ground any perp who dared take to his heels. Old Man Lehman was lucky to have me for a partner.

I cut to the chase. "Leads?"

"Nothing."

"Anybody report their key card missing?" Neither the door into the garage nor the one to the downstairs hallway had been forced; someone had used a key card. Which meant either one of our staff was missing one—or worse; one of our own officers had attacked Steph Buchanan.

Lehman looked past me to the parking lot and ran his tongue over his teeth thoughtfully. "I got a funny feeling someone's *about* to report a key card missing."

I turned. A tiny red Chevy two-door, the kind of just-functional junker you got saddled with in college, swerved into a stall and jerked to a halt. The door sprang open and Chad Rauch stepped out, a striking contrast to his ride. He wasn't on the schedule today, yet he was dressed head-to-toe in uniform, hat and all, every scrap of leather and metal polished to a high shine, black hair freshly buzzed. I was pretty sure military experience wasn't in his past, but, damn, it could have been. A smart young professional like that deserved a better set of wheels.

He walked straight up to us, shoulders square, hat tucked smartly under his arm. He looked Lehman straight in the eye—addressing him not because Lehman was male and technically outranked me, but because the new recruits were well aware my wrath was not to be tampered with. Despite turning to the more lenient of his superiors, his face was bloodless.

"Detective Sergeant Lehman, sir," he said.

Lehman worked his jaw and tapped his notebook against his thigh. "You lost a key card, didn't you?"

The boy's face melted like wax that had been warming in the sun, the gooey innards finally spilling through the fake outer shell. He suddenly looked like the twenty-one-year-old kid he was. On second thought, he totally deserved the junker. "Yes, sir," he said, and for a moment, I thought he might actually cry. He'd only been signed off by his Field Training Officer last week.

"How'd you lose it?" Lehman asked.

Rauch took a shaky breath and motioned with his hands as if wading through a marsh. "I-I don't know," he stammered. "I had it yesterday. Today it's gone."

Lehman sighed and nodded patiently. "Well, go check your locker before you run around confessing sins." He pushed off the wall, pulled open the door, and waved Rauch through.

The boy's face dawned with hope. "My locker. Yes, sir." He bounced on his heels then charged through the door.

"Five bucks says it isn't in his locker," Lehman commented when he was gone.

"I'll keep my five," I countered. I pushed my hands into my hips, stretching my back. "Well, wherever that missing key card is, we have a bigger question on our hands."

"What the perp wanted?"

I nodded. "He went straight to the records room. He wanted info on a case. An old case. But which one?"

Lehman's face crumpled into a pout that looked pathetic on a forty-year-old man. "I have a bad feeling I know where this is going."

I grinned and pulled a key from my pocket—a good, old-fashioned metal one—and held it up, its teeth catching sunlight. During our initial processing of the records storage room, nothing had looked obviously out of place. But maybe the perpetrator had left a folder sticking out. A page dog-eared. I shifted an inviting eyebrow at Lehman. "Ready to sift through fifty years of paper records with me?" The tenacious dog had latched onto its next victim.

Lehman ground his palms into his eyes. "Oh, God, shoot me now."

CHAPTER FOUR
TOMMY

Settled into my captain's chair, I drummed my fingers on the worn wood of the helm. Classic, big-band jazz crooned over the sound system while the passengers behind me chatted and laughed at their linen-draped tables, spoons clinking on crystal bowls. The broad windshield of the Mailboat gave me a panoramic view of the lake; on a Monday morning, the water was calm as a painting. The rambling old mansions of the North Shore gazed silently, most of the homeowners at work in Chicago for the week.

I sighed. It was too quiet around here. Our client, hosting a business outing from Racine, had requested a cruise with no tour. Otherwise, one of the kids would be sitting on the tall stool next to me to read the well-thumbed script. Those who had worked several summers barely glanced at it anymore. I hadn't touched it in forty-odd years.

Tomorrow, a dozen kids would take their turns in the mail jumper's chair, some for the first time. Both pedestal and podium, it would be the focus of attention while the candidates were judged for their skills in presentation. But first, the white-painted piers would serve as stage for our cast of fleet-footed actors. I never knew who I'd end up working with, though jumpers from past years were generally a shoe-in. For the newbies, I'd give my two cents on who was ready for the job and who wasn't, but the decision was ultimately in the hands of the boss and a few honorary judges—people who had jumped mail while I was still in rompers, or so I doggedly maintained. These three or four individuals dictated who kept me company the rest of the summer and who went back to selling tickets.

By and large, I believed in letting the waves bring to shore whatever they may. The currents of life flowed too strong for those of us caught up in it to protest the details. Still, there was one kid I hoped would make the team this year...

I turned in my seat to sight down the aisle between the tables, up the short flight of stairs, and straight to the aft deck. I could just see the concessions counter. Bailey sat behind it, chin in her palm, strands of wavy brown hair escaping her pony tail as they usually did, the lake humidity playing its favorite game with her. She stared blankly at the countertop while twirling an ice cream scoop in a bowl.

The tables had all been served. The passengers were happy. And my mail jumper's chair was empty. No point Bailey sitting back there bored.

I picked up a microphone, lying within arm's reach on the counter beside the helm. My voice sounded over the jazz music. "Bailey, will you come fore, please?"

I waited for her to look up, but she continued twirling the ice cream scoop as if she hadn't heard me. I was about to page her again when she jolted in her seat, as if the speed of sound had slowed considerably from what I learned in school. Her eyes, round as a kitten's, flashed up and stared down the length of the boat. Finding me looking at her, she pointed to herself, raising her eyebrows.

I laughed. Typical of Bailey, so lost in her own world that there was a delay between her ears and her head. In confirmation to her pantomimed question, I jerked my head towards the bow.

She slid off her stool behind the snack bar, jogged down the stairs, and scurried up the aisle. "Yes?" she asked, eyes still wide. I swore, half the time she thought she was in trouble.

"Grab a seat," I said, slapping the backrest of the mail jumper's chair.

Obediently, she hopped onto the high stool, tucking her hands under her thighs. Her seat conveniently faced the deck where she could keep an eye on the passengers while I faced forward, reading the surface of the lake.

"Yes?" she said again, like the freshest of seaman recruits eager to be issued her orders.

Well, so long as she thought I'd brought her here for a purpose, I may as well play along. Nothing wrong with putting kids to honest work. "You practiced that script yet?" I nodded to the white ring binder on the counter, smudged black at the edges from countless fingers.

"Practiced?" she echoed. Her face hadn't lost the look of a tarsier, eyes impossibly round.

"You're trying out for mail jumper tomorrow, aren't you?"

She nodded. "Yes, sir."

"It's Tommy," I corrected, then bit my tongue before the mantra of every NCO in the Navy could spring to my lips: *Don't call me "sir"; I work for a living.* The title *sir* was reserved for commissioned officers—something I had never been. The captain's bars now perched on my shoulders were only an honorific, by my reckoning.

"Huh?" she asked.

"You can call me Tommy," I repeated. "It's what everybody calls me."

She nodded her head. "Yes, sir."

I looked out the side window and ran a hand over my mouth to smother laughter. At all times, Bailey marched a beat behind the band and I had to admit, it humored me. Yes, I'd be very disappointed if she didn't make the team.

I'd fought hard to learn how to laugh again. I forgot how after I lost my son and my wife within a few years of each other. But even now, laughter felt forced. A barricade. If you acted all right, people thought you were all right. They never probed into the disappointments, the hurt, the anger that lay just below the mirrored surface.

But something about Bailey's world was upside-down, inside-out. She constantly caught me off guard, surprised me. I laughed freely around her, the way I used to long ago.

"So," I tried again, "did you practice the script?"

"Oh!" she squeaked. "I didn't know I was supposed to." Twisting in her seat, she grabbed the binder off the counter, plopped it into her lap, and flipped to the beginning. As she crouched over the book, her eyes flashed back and forth over the text, lips muttering, as she read to herself and not to me.

She was taut as a hawser. In her eagerness to please, she'd probably send all her chances marching right off the end of the plank—a risk I couldn't let her take. "Sit up straight," I coached.

She sprang to attention without pausing for breath or taking her eyes from the book.

"Slow down. Breathe a little."

She closed her lips and breathed in deeply through her nose. Then she began to read out loud in a steady, clear voice. "'The Prairie-style building behind the park is the Lake Geneva Public Library, designed by James Dresser, a student of Frank Lloyd Wright.'"

I grinned, proud of how quickly she'd improved. "Good," I said. "Look at the passengers now and again."

She paused, mouth open, and flashed her eyes toward the tables. The chatter didn't abate, and without the use of the microphone it was safe to assume the men and women in business suits hadn't so much as noticed her. Still, as if intimidated by what she saw, she dropped her eyes immediately to the page. Her voice lost volume and wavered. "'The land and the original building were donated by—'"

"You're not worried, are you?" I asked.

Bailey's shoulders slouched as if she were visibly curling up inside herself. She nodded.

Something in my chest twinged for her. The way it had when my son had worried about making the high school football team. He'd turned out to be a darn good running back, despite my hopes he'd sign up for baseball. I never did understand the brutish sport of chasing the pigskin, but it had been a passion of his so I let him have his way in the end. I hadn't attended a lot of games, though.

I looked away and licked my lips. "You'll do fine," I said, remembering now that I'd never said those words to my son. His worries had been my worries—but he never knew it. I didn't let it show. I was a stubborn old curmudgeon back then. I still was. I watched the shore again, hoping Bailey wouldn't see me lost in memories—the kind submerged for years, covered in barnacles, razor-sharp.

She placed her finger in her page and closed the binder. "Tommy?" she asked. "How did they break in?"

I leaned closer, straining my ears. "What's that?" As usual, she was leaping from one bar of music to the next and I couldn't keep up.

"The police station," she said, her voice so low I could barely hear. She turned large brown eyes on me. "How'd they break in?"

For being so busy spinning her own tune, she apparently took in more of mine than I thought. She must have overheard my conversation this morning with Wade Erickson, the police chief and an old friend of mine. I'd promised to pass along any info the kids knew—but I had to admit, Bailey was the last person I'd thought would have any connection.

"I don't know how they broke in," I said. "I imagine that information's classified."

She narrowed her eyes suspiciously. "Classified?"

Well, that did make it sound like a spy thriller. "There's always something the police hold back from public knowledge," I said, a fact I'd learned from Wade. "That way, they can confirm whether they've got the right person once they take in a suspect."

"Oh." She scrunched her nose in contemplation. "So... what happens when someone—you know, like a member of the public—thinks they know something?"

I slid my eyes her direction. Shoulders rounded, she frowned down at the binder. There was only one reason she'd ask such a question. "You should call the police station," I said pointedly.

She morphed back into the tarsier, as if the thought of calling the police frightened her more than addressing the passengers while reading the script.

I shifted in my seat to face her and studied the side of her face. Wisps of mousy brown hair framed her cheeks like a curtain. "Bailey, what do you know?"

"Nothing, really." I was about to mark it as a lie, but then she lifted her head and looked at me. There was no deceit. Just worry and confusion. "What if I'm wrong? What if I get someone in trouble?"

Well, that was a fair enough concern for a teenage girl. I thought back to my own teen years. No doubt calling the police would feel like tattling. Like watching a sibling get grounded because you said something. I wondered if she knew just how serious this thing was—that Steph Buchanan spent her morning in the hospital, but could just as easily have been killed. I sighed and cast my gaze over the rolling blue waves. "The police will want to know anyway. They can sort out whether the information is relevant or not."

She dropped her gaze into her lap and nodded.

I cast a glance her way. How could Bailey of all people have gotten dragged into this? "Who are you afraid of getting into trouble?" I asked.

She only bit her lips together and shook her head.

"You won't tell me?"

She studied the warped edges of the binder in silence. Shook her head again.

I sighed and grabbed a worn old envelope off the counter and wrote on it. "Here," I said. "That's the number to the police station." I'd known Chief Wade Erickson since he was a rookie—longer. As such, I'd memorized the number to the station long before there were smart phones. I inserted the paper between Bailey's thumb and the binder. "Call them." It wasn't a suggestion.

Bailey nodded.

I studied her downcast face. She was too young to worry about things like break-ins, assaults, police investigations. Her mind should be filled with the future, with possibility, with opportunity. What she wanted to study next fall. What she wanted to study in college. What career she wanted to go into. And yes, whether she'd make the mail jumping team tomorrow. But the question now stuck in her head seemed to weigh her down like an anchor on a line too short to reach the bottom. I couldn't stand to see her this way.

"Go on," I said, nodding at the binder. "'The land and the original building for the library were donated by...?'"

Bailey straightened her back and flipped open the book. She resumed her clear, steady voice. "'The land and the original building were donated by Mary Sturges, with the understanding that they would remain a public park and library forever...'"

I let the well-known words sink into my soul, shaded in the tones of a new young voice. I'd weathered storms, losses, nightmares. I'd learned to let the waves wash ashore whatever they may, to watch with disinterest, to pretend to laugh.

I couldn't pretend I didn't care whether Bailey made the team.

CHAPTER FIVE
MONICA

My hands encased in nitrile gloves, I pulled out one cardboard box after another, peeled off the lids, and flipped through the contents. There was no way to tell whether a record was missing aside from checking each and every call-for-service number from each and every year, including our earliest documents—yellowing pages dated to the 1960s.

It was the kind of tedious work my undiagnosed OCD delighted in.

A few feet down the row, Lehman shoved a box back onto its shelf. "Did you know a cow got loose downtown in 1968?"

"That so?" I asked, my eyes and fingers scanning numbers.

"Yep. Farmer Willard Tillman's cow. Name of Annabelle, a doe-eyed Jersey who made the best cheese in four counties. They herded her onto the Riviera Pier where she jumped off and swam ashore, right into her daddy's waiting arms—well, his trailer, anyway."

"Good for her."

Lehman sighed and leaned against a shelf. "You're welcome, by the way."

"For what?"

"Helping you with this. Rock-turning is your department. I'm more of an interviews and interrogations guy; you know that."

"That's only because people couldn't hate your ass any more than they already do." Prying away at people's secrets didn't win you friends. "And I might point out, you have no one to interrogate until we pick up a lead."

"Touché."

I waved to the next shelf. "Nineteen sixty-nine is waiting."

He sighed and pulled out another box, cardboard sliding on particle board and metal. "You've seen the security footage. The perp couldn't have been in here more than five minutes before Steph showed up. He didn't have a chance to find whatever he was after."

"You don't know that."

He leaned his arm on the shelving. "Why do you always consider the impossible to be the likely?"

"You're the one who told me a cow dove off the Riviera Pier."

He hung his head and shook it side-to-side. "I wish I hadn't told you that."

Lehman was the big-picture guy. I was into the details. In theory, that should have made us a great team. Instead, we were trapped in a constant push-pull, one of us railroading the other into whatever we wanted. I usually won, but Lehman spent the rest of the time griping.

An hour later, our fingers flying through the nineties, Lehman was singing just loud enough for me to hear. "Oh, bury me not... Under lock and key... Where paperwork howls... And reports blow free..."

He'd been improvising lyrics for the past fifteen minutes and I was ready to cram a box over his head. A scathing comment about to fly off my tongue, I bit it short as my eye finally caught what I'd been looking for.

A loose sheet of paper, half out of its box, torn at the corner where a staple used to be.

I pulled the sheet free. The header on top listed the date as August 29th, 1995, the page number as three of three. The print-out began mid-sentence, the first sheet missing from the report.

...resisted arrest by refusing to follow orders and struggling as I attempted to put on the handcuffs. Officer Steele arrived at the scene at this time and assisted and we then were able to contain the subject. The subject was identified via his driver's license as Roger Ridley Holland. His rights were read to him at this time...

My eyes flashed to the signature at the bottom of the report. Sergeant Horace Stubbs.

"Oh, my God," I breathed.

The cop's version of the cowboy lament died mid-verse. "What?" Lehman asked.

"Oh, shit."

He shoved his box back onto the shelf and came to peer over my shoulder. "What? What is it?"

I passed him the torn report. He scanned the type-written text. "The Holland Murder," he said, all business now.

"Murder?" I repeated. "Really, Lehman?" I felt the heat rising beneath my collar.

Lehman tilted an eyebrow at me. "Yes, Monica. So said a jury of his peers in a court of law."

I jabbed a finger at the signature. "So said Sergeant Stubbs, you mean."

Lehman raised his hands, one of them holding the torn page. "Whoa, whoa, whoa, let's dial this down a notch."

"Dial it down a notch?" I spat out. "I nearly lost my job over Stubbs." I pointed out a line from the report. 'Officer Steele'—that's me. And look—remember this?"

I stormed around the corner to a set of shelves against the wall, old personnel files. I'd been a stark rookie in 1995, still in my first year of probation, barely sturdy enough to carry a ballistic vest and duty belt without crumpling under the weight. I was finally a full-time cop, and I'd staked my fledgling career to blow the whistle. In Stubbs' folder, I knew I'd find my own written complaint—the one the lieutenant had brushed over. The one that had earmarked me as an over-zealous greenhorn. In that complaint, I had accused Stubbs of knowingly disturbing the crime scene. Of fabricating evidence. Of framing Roger Holland for murder instead of the accidental death it was. Holland was a baker, for God's sake, not a murderer. The victim had been his best friend.

I pulled out a box marked with the letter *S* and pawed for Stubbs' file. A moment later, my hands froze.

"It's gone," I said, disbelief filling my voice. "Stubbs' personnel file. The whole thing. It's gone." I felt as robbed as I had the day my lieutenant told me, *Yes, I've seen your complaint and filed it appropriately.*

Lehman glanced at the torn report in his hand. "I guess we know what the perp was after, then. Info on the Holland case."

I looked at my partner over my shoulder. "Where's Roger Holland now?"

Lehman shrugged. "Still up at the state pen, I think. They gave him life. But he'd be an old man now. What about Stubbs? Where's he?"

"Door County," I replied. "Retired to some cabin on the peninsula."

"Should I be disturbed you know that?" Lehman asked, hoisting an eyebrow.

I glared daggers at him. "I never take my eyes off a dirty cop. Especially one that got away."

Lehman rolled his head dismissively. "Monica, you could never prove he did it—or even why he'd want to."

"Sergeant Stubbs liked making things easy," I shot back. "Too easy. Why let the jury hang on murder versus accidental death when it could just be a nice, clean murder? He sentenced Roger Holland himself the night he walked onto the scene."

Lehman raised his hands again. "Okay, okay, let's not drudge up all the bad feelings right now. The important thing is, we've got leads." He lifted the ripped sheet still in his gloved hand and waved at it. "Maybe we even have fingerprints. We know what our burglar came for. The only question now is why."

"Holland's raising a new appeal," I said.

Lehman raised his eyebrows. "He is?"

"I don't know. But he could be. And Stubbs wants the records conveniently erased. He wants no evidence that Holland could use against him." I jabbed a thumb at myself. "He wants *my* record of complaint to disappear."

"Or," Lehman countered, "Holland's raising a new appeal and needs this evidence."

I shook my head, frowning. "His lawyer would be nuts. He could simply file a request for the police report."

"The report, yes," Lehman agreed, "but the personnel file?"

"So he stole it? I don't buy that. Stubbs, on the other hand... I worked with him, remember? He was so rotten inside, he stank. Plants shriveled when he walked by."

Lehman sighed. "Much as I enjoy discussing semantics..." He took down the *S* box from the shelf, placed it in my gloved hands, and laid the torn report on the lid. "This isn't our baby anymore. It's all getting turned over to D.C.I. now."

The Wisconsin Department of Criminal Investigations. We weren't allowed to investigate one of our own cops, even if he was retired. Conflicts of interest were the reason why—like my keen desire to turn Stubbs' spine into a twisty-tie and shove his head up his own ass.

I blew a strand of hair out of my face. "They better do it right. I catch one whiff of any half-assed police work, and I'll have their badges."

Lehman rolled his eyes. "Monica, your half-ass is an ass and a half to anyone else."

I raised an eyebrow. "Watch it, buster, or I'll have *you* for sexual harassment."

"Sexual harassment. Right." He turned me around by the shoulders and dug his index fingers into my back, nudging me towards the door and the evidence collection room down the hall. "You go stow those in evidence. I'll call D.C.I."

TUESDAY
JUNE 11, 2013

CHAPTER SIX
BAILEY

I was gonna throw up. I couldn't do this. I wasn't cut out to be a mail jumper.

Pacing the quay behind the Riviera, I watched the kids gather on the pier a few paces away. There was the boss. The judges. The people from the TV stations and the newspapers—they never missed the annual appointment of the famous Lake Geneva mail jumpers. I swung my arms and clapped my palms together while sucking air through my lips. This was it. Go time. I needed to get out there and join the show. It was time to do this thing!

I couldn't. I planted my back against one of the brick pillars and buried my face in my hands.

It was lousy weather for your first try at mail jumping. Woolly gray clouds hung low in the sky, occasionally spitting a little mist. The boards beneath my feet were dappled with water, as would be every pier around the lake. What if my shoes didn't stick? What if I fell and broke my nose? My arm? My neck?

What if I didn't make the team?

Out on the pier, a reporter pushed a microphone towards Tommy. I was just close enough to overhear.

"Are you going to take it easy on the newbies today?" I recognized the reporter as Tim Fairchild from WISN12. Another man standing behind him balanced a camera on his shoulder.

"Nah," Tommy said. "The run will do them good." He chuckled.

I stared at Tommy and felt a big, hungry hole in the pit of my stomach. Like when you haven't had a bar of chocolate in forever 'cause your foster parents save them all for the two-year-old 'cause *he's so darn cute!* and for some reason you've developed a ravenous craving for chocolate. I just wanted something good to happen in my life for once, you know?

A voice spoke behind me. "You came."

I jumped and whirled. Baron Hackett smiled, his arm casually thrown up against a brick pillar, his other hand hooked through the strap of his backpack. Like all the kids, like me, he was wearing navy shorts and a white polo shirt bearing the logo of the cruise line company. The cowrie shell on his necklace peeked out from between his collars and the diamond stud glittered in his ear.

"Uh... yeah," I squeaked. "Yeah, I came." *Why did you have that key card to the police station?* I swallowed hard and hoped my skull wasn't see-through.

He smiled—the kind of grin that would convince millions of the TV-viewing public to buy whatever aftershave he was advertising. "You'll do fine," he said with raised eyebrows and a big nod.

Was it that obvious I was nervous? Was my face green? Oh, God, maybe my skull *was* see-through...

"Look, uh..." He shuffled his feet uncertainly. I'd never thought Baron could feel uncertain. What was wrong? He was all but guaranteed a spot on the team. "I don't actually know if I'll be around much this summer."

I frowned. "Then why are you trying out?"

He shrugged. "Wishful thinking, maybe?" He grinned at me, a lop-sided smile that was sad and heartbreakingly beautiful all at once. His secretive, magical eyes connected with mine. Delved into my very soul. Searched me. Searched *for* me.

My heart turned into a chunk of ice, sending frozen tendrils into every extremity of my body. What was he saying? Why was he looking at me like that? Did he... Oh, God, did he *like* me?

My brain screamed that I didn't have an acceptance letter from Harvard, a requirement for any girl before she could be noticed by Baron Hackett, much less liked by him. What was he thinking? Couldn't he see the school newspaper headlines? *Prince Falls for Pauper—Hackett, Johnson a Couple?!*

I shook my head and stepped back from him.

Baron's face fell. "What's the matter?"

I stared at him wide-eyed. This didn't feel right. Nobody liked me. Nobody even liked me enough to keep me. Invisibility was the only world I knew how to function in. But how did you tell the king of Badger High to stuff it?

Worse, how did you tell him you thought maybe he was the one who broke into the police station? But of course I'd never say that. I hadn't even built up the courage yet to call the number Tommy had given me.

"Uh..." My mouth felt like sand. I glanced toward the Mailboat. "They're starting," I said, relieved for an out. "We should go."

He followed my gaze. Saw the kids stepping away from the reporters and gathering around our boss. Baron looked into my eyes again. He must have felt the wall of ice there 'cause he backed off. "You're right," he replied, and it was probably the nicest thing anyone had ever said to me.

We fell into step side-by-side but with an awkward, wonderful space between us. Baron's stride was straight and strong like always, as if nothing had happened. I was pretty sure I wobbled down the pier like a top running out of spin.

I reached into my pocket and touched a wad of paper, folded up into a tiny square. The envelope Tommy had given me with the number to the police station. Why did I have to be the one sucked into this whirlpool? Why was I the one who had to make this decision?

CHAPTER SEVEN
MONICA

I plopped into a chair, the vinyl seat packed hard by countless butts, and tore the wrapper off my breakfast burrito. I bit into the soft outer shell. Eggs and sausage hit my tongue while the torn edge of the burrito steamed. My breakfast choice matched my mood. With the case out of my hands now, I burned inside. I wanted to see Horace Stubbs earn his dues and I wanted to see someone pay for assaulting Steph Buchanan.

"Any news from D.C.I.?" I asked my partner.

Lehman poked a fork into a giant blueberry muffin. "They arrested Stubbs last night."

I bolted upright in my chair. "What?" Now *that* was what I called police work. I was ready to get on the phone right then and commend the investigating detectives to their superiors.

"No," said Lehman, grinning behind another mound of muffin, "but I couldn't help getting a rise out of you."

I bared my teeth. "I'll murder you."

"Eh, I've been on your hit list for years." He sipped his Triple Chocolate Mocha. "Seriously, what did you expect? We only handed the case over yesterday."

"I know." Leaning on my elbows, I brooded over my burrito. "I just can't stand not knowing what's going on."

He shook his head, pulling a long, mournful face. "Patience was never one of your virtues."

I lifted an eyebrow at him, unmoved by his observation.

"How about fishing? You should try it." He set his fork down and swallowed. "Mm. I caught this walleye last night..." He tapped his forefingers on the table about three feet apart, a boyish grin lighting up his face.

"You know there's only one way I'd ever go fishing," I said, keeping my eyes bland. "Barrel, Glock." I made a hand motion as if firing a gun and mouthed a shooting noise.

Lehman stared in blank horror. He glanced away to release a small burp, and with it, no doubt, some of his shock at my idea of angling. "Wow, that's bloody."

I grabbed a fork and stabbed it into my burrito, filling it with holes, my appetite vanished. "What if D.C.I. doesn't find enough evidence?" I fretted.

Lehman was still staring vacantly. "All those fillets, just..." He turned up his palms. "Mangled."

I slapped my fork down on the table. "I'm serious, Lehman. What if Stubbs walks free all over again?" I dug my fingers into my hair, nails baring down on my scalp. "My God, I would die. And right now, he's the only lead we've got on Steph's attack."

Lehman sighed, as if mentally saying a few moving words to the slaughtered fish before laying them to rest. Only then did he poke his muffin again and shrug. "Someone will report something on the burglar."

I turned angry eyes on him. "No one's going to report anything. We don't even have a decent picture of the perp to share on social media."

Lehman grinned sarcastically. "Well, maybe we can round up a few suspects into a barrel and you can shoot them."

I frowned. "You're not going to let that one drop, are you?"

"Some images can never be erased." Lehman sipped more mocha. "Seriously, Monica, quit worrying about it. The break this investigation needs is right around the corner." He popped the last bite of muffin into his mouth and pointed at me with his fork. "Just you see."

CHAPTER EIGHT
BAILEY

Woo! Yeah!

Whoops, hollers, and applause erupted as Melissa Kraft landed gracefully on the rub board. She shook out her glorious locks, brown with blond highlights, and strolled the narrow catwalk back towards the bow without so much as holding the hand rail. Her shoes hadn't skidded once on the wet pier. She hadn't fumbled for a second with the mail or the mailbox. Was it really as easy as she made it look? Then again, she was a junior in college who'd been jumping mail for six years. There was a good chance she actually knew what she was doing.

The other candidates sat in a cluster of white plastic chairs in the middle of the deck, Baron among them. Sitting crooked, he used an armrest for a backrest and the backrest for an armrest. He looked all casual. Assured. Confident. Like Melissa, it was inconceivable he wouldn't make the team. But he listened to the other kids cavort without joining the conversation. The veterans verbally jockeyed for the worst prank ever played on a jumper: mailboxes tied shut with rubber bands, obstacle courses built out of deck furniture, and piers covered in fresh, white paint—not really a prank, but not fun, either, if you slipped and ended up with a white bum for the rest of the day.

The first-timers listened wide-eyed. Maybe mail jumping was more hazardous than we thought.

Sitting at the rear of the group, my back against the side of the boat, I listened and pretended to text on my phone. Hopefully no one knew I had no one to text with. But none of them noticed me. Thank God. Between Baron and tryouts, my brain was silently trying to explode.

The TV reporter, the one who had talked to Tommy, scanned the group and noticed I wasn't busy yammering with the others. He slipped into a chair beside me. "Tim Fairchild, WISN12," he said, sticking out his hand. "What's your name?"

I eyed his hand suspiciously but wasn't quite rude enough to reject it. Still, I didn't put any heart into my grip—if you could call it that. "I'm Bailey," I said.

"Is this your first time?" he asked.

I glared at the mic in his other hand, wanting to say *no* just so he'd go away. But given a direct question, I was pathetic at giving cagey answers. "Y-y-yeah?" I dragged the word out like a question, and that was the best I could do.

His grin spread ear-to-ear, like he'd struck gold or something. "Is it okay if we get an interview?"

"Uh..." I lifted a shoulder in a shrug, waiting for my brain to drum up an excuse.

But the reporter mistook the shrug for an okay. "Great, thanks. Clint!"

The cameraman scurried over, popped out a tripod, and secured his electronic contraption to the top. "Rolling," he muttered, his face glued to an eyepiece.

The reporter pushed his mic next to my mouth. "What's your full name?"

"Um... Bailey Johnson."

"Will you spell it for the camera, please?"

44

I did.

"Bailey, this is your first time trying out. What are you feeling?"

I stared blankly at Tim Fairchild, wondering why the universe was such an asshole. Out of all the questions he could have asked, why the one I was in no mood to talk about? With *anyone?* Much less with half the population of *Wisconsin?*

Well, Mr. Fairchild, I kind of feel like tying dumbbells to my ankles and throwing myself into the deepest part of the lake. I'm sure that's a normal feeling for first-time mail jumpers, right?

Fortunately, none of that was what came out of my mouth.

"A little nervous," was what I said.

"What's your biggest fear?"

How about suffering through three more years of high school with the stigma of having ratted out the most popular boy at Badger High? I could already see it now: The hate notes slipped into my locker. The books being knocked out of my hands on my way to every class. The grassroots campaign to make every minute of my life as miserable as possible. The fact that *literally everybody* would know who I was. Would be staring at me, noticing me, and while they were at it, *hating* me. I would be as un-invisible as a pile of dog poo in the middle of a banquet table.

But no. Being noticed, known, and hated by my whole school wasn't even the thing I feared most right now. I glanced up the boat at Tommy, standing at the helm, his back to me. That's what I was afraid of. I was afraid of Tommy standing with his back to me for the rest of the summer. For the rest of my life. I was afraid of being completely, utterly alone. A piece of forgotten driftwood. The unwanted kid. Like I had been my whole life.

Tim Fairchild's question was still waiting for an answer.

"I mean, slipping and falling off a pier would be pretty bad," I lied.

"Oo, yeah, that would hurt," the reporter said.

Yeah. Sure. But not as bad as the stuff I was actually afraid of. Not as much as the life I'd already been living for fifteen years.

"How do you think you'll do today?" the reporter went on. "Are you going to make the team?" He cocked his head towards the starboard side of the boat, where another jumper was getting ready out on the catwalk, an envelope in his hand.

Quit making it sound like it's so much fun, I wanted to snap. *This is hard. I don't know what I'll do if I don't make the team.* But an answer like that wouldn't have made any sense.

I shrugged. "I guess we'll find out."

The reporter lowered the mic, giving me hope this interview of torture was over. "Well, good luck today, Bailey."

I forced a smile. "Thanks." Personally, I thought all my answers—the out-loud ones—were boring and dumb. Maybe I'd be lucky and they'd toss the entire interview on the cutting room floor instead of putting it on the evening news.

Tim Fairchild and his cameraman stood up. "Here," Tim said, "Why don't we get some shots of this…?" They walked away.

When I looked around, Baron Hackett was staring right at me. His face was blank. He'd probably just been watching the interview. But I felt as if I were made of glass and he could see every angle of my soul—including all the answers I'd kept to myself.

I jumped out of my chair and hurried toward the back, pretending I had to go to the bathroom. I tucked myself into the tiny closet, pulled the pocket door shut behind me, and latched the hook and eye lock. I closed the lid to the toilet and sat on it, burying my face in my hands. I let the tears fall. This was too hard. And I was so alone.

No, I wasn't. The engines of the Mailboat rumbled below my feet. I could feel them through the floorboards, a great purr like a lion wrapping me up in its velvety paws, nesting my head in its silky mane. *There, there, child. I'm here. I'm always here.*

When I was down to only sniffles, I pulled the square of paper out of my pocket. Unfolded it. Stared down at the phone number written in Tommy's blocky handwriting. It was so dumb, how badly I just wanted to be around him more. To always feel the way I did when he was near. Calm. Happy. Peaceful. Not terrified of literally everything. As courageous as a child wrapped safely in a lion's paws.

You should call the police station, he'd said. His tone had left no room for argument. This was what he expected of me. He would have told me it didn't matter what the other kids at school thought of me, turning in their favorite classmate. It didn't even matter if the teachers were mad, digging up the dirt on their star pupil. Tommy expected me to do the right thing, no matter how hard it was.

I pulled out my phone, woke it up, and checked my reception, which was always spotty on the lake. If I had two bars or less, I wouldn't do it.

There were three bars. Dumb phone.

I glared daggers at the treacherous little icon in the upper right corner. Then I locked my jaws and pulled up the call app. I typed in the number and hit *send* before I could stop myself.

The line picked up almost immediately. "Lake Geneva Police Department," a woman's voice said on the other end.

Butterflies raced in giddy circles round and round my stomach. "Um, hi. I wanted to call in... um... It's something to do with the break-in the other night. At the police station."

"You wanted to report information?" the woman asked. Without losing the professional overtone, she sounded the tiniest bit eager.

"Yeah."

"One moment. Let me put you through to the detective's bureau."

No, don't put me on hold, I wanted to say. *What if I hang up before you guys pick up again? Do you have any idea how hard it was to work up the nerve?*

But instead, I heard myself say, "Thanks."

The line clicked subtly, rang twice, then clicked again.

"Detective Steele."

It was another woman's voice. This one was brusque. Clipped. The voice of someone who'd worn the badge of authority long enough to have zero tolerance for bullshit. Someone who would tan Baron Hackett's hide, hang it out to dry, then go grab a sammy for lunch—no chips, but I'll take avocado.

"Uh, hi." I stared at the bathroom door, suddenly finding the flowy patters of the woodgrain fascinating. Behind me, tiny raindrops tapped on the window. The engines continued to hum, offering their unwavering support, as if Tommy himself were watching over my shoulder, encouraging me on. "I wanted to report something about the break-in at the police station."

"Who am I speaking to, please?"

I bit my lip. "Can I, like, report anonymously?"

"Absolutely," the woman said. "Your name will be withheld from public record. However, I need your name and contact information in case I need to follow up with you after this phone call."

"Oh." Her assurance that no one would know I was the one who'd tattled didn't help. I couldn't erase the images of the whole school staring me down in the hallways, glaring, turning the cold shoulder. I didn't think I could survive being hated by literally everyone.

I took a deep breath and did one of the few daring things I've ever done. I ignored the detective's instructions and skipped ahead to the important part.

"You need to talk to Baron Hackett," I said, my voice wavering. "He's a student at Badger High. Oh, and he works at the cruise line. He..." *He has a key card. He broke into the police station.* I couldn't bring myself to say any of that. "He knows stuff," I finally settled, my voice nearly breaking in two. "'Kay, that's it."

"Wait—"

But I'd already taken the phone away from my ear. I stared at the little red phone icon, telling myself not to do it. And then I did it. I punched the button and ended the call.

And then I just sat there shaking, my stomach doing back flips. Thank God the toilet was handy.

A rap sounded on the door.

My eyes shot to the latch. My brain conjured images of Baron pounding on the other side. *Bailey Johnson, I know what you've done!*

But the voice that called through the door wasn't Baron's.

"Yo, Bailey, you're up!"

It was Melissa Kraft.

"I'm coming!" I called back, my voice shaking, relief and fear hitting me at once. Thank God, Baron didn't know. But I was supposed to go out there now and not kill myself delivering mail. Maybe I should just fall in the lake and never come up.

Melissa's footsteps walked away.

I folded in half over my arms and let the shudders run up and down my body. What had I done? How was I supposed to get through what I had to do next?

CHAPTER NINE
MONICA

Shit!

I called into the handset—"Hello? Hello?"—but the girl was gone. So I hung up and dialed the Communications Center. While it rang, I rapped a pen and stared at the wall of my cubicle. Nothing but a fuzzy gray backdrop, it was utterly devoid of photos, sticky notes, or (God forbid) succulents in tiny hanging vases. A clean space fostered a clear mind.

"Angie," I said when the telecommunicator picked up, "what's the phone number on that call you sent up to me?"

"Just a sec." Angie was silent while her computer mouse clicked in the background. "Oh… Oops."

Oops? What did *oops* mean? "What?"

"Um… I must have picked up too fast. The number didn't have a chance to register."

I braced my elbow on my desk and pinched the bridge of my nose. Angie had been working here for nine years. What was she doing making rookie mistakes?

"Sorry, Steele," she said, and I could hear her bracing for a tongue lashing.

"It's okay," I sighed. It wasn't. But I didn't have time for tirades. "Thanks for checking."

"Of course."

I hung up. "Shit!"

Lehman rolled away from his desk and peered around the divider between our cubicles. His, I knew, was littered with pics of his kids at various ages—his ex conveniently excluded—and magazine clippings of sports cars he'd never be able to afford. "What's wrong?" he asked.

"We've got a lead." I flipped open my portfolio and scribbled notes from the all-too-brief conversation.

Lehman spread his arms. "What'd I tell you! Someone had to know something."

"Yeah, but I don't have the PR's contact info."

"Oh. Well, shit," Lehman agreed.

I ripped the sheet from my notebook and handed it to him. "Call D.C.I. and pass that on to them." I turned to my computer and pulled up our driver's license database, clacking my keyboard furiously.

Lehman stuck on a pair of reading glasses and stared at my note. "So, our anonymous PR could provide evidence that this—" he frowned at my note "—Baron Hackett was the one who broke in?"

"No. She didn't even accuse him of anything. She just said, 'He knows stuff.'" I lifted my hands from my keyboard long enough to make air quotes. "But she was hella nervous. I think she was afraid of saying too much."

"Hmm. Well, I'll pass it on." He pushed off and rolled back to his own desk. His phone clicked out of its cradle.

"Wait," I said.

"What?"

I was staring at the info I needed. A search for Baron's driver's license had brought up his home address. From there, I'd hopped over to the county's database of properties and found the owner.

"Tell D.C.I. they might want to be careful," I said. "Looks like his dad's Richard Hackett."

"Who?" Lehman demanded from the other side of the divider. Most of our conversations took place with a wall between us, and I liked it better that way.

"Richard Hackett," I said. "He moved his family here about a year ago." I studied the map provided by the county property database. "Apparently they have one of the big houses on the South Shore. Hackett originally made his fortune in Silicon Valley. Then his daughter had a career in Hollywood. That's why they moved here, to get away from the hype. Now Hackett's an angel investor."

"Geez, what do you do, read the social column?"

"No, politics. Hackett's running for the county board of supervisors."

"Shit, do we have an election this fall?"

I rolled my eyes, leaned against the back of my chair, and spoke to the ceiling. "The point is, with Hackett's background, he's used to playing in the Big Leagues. The moment D.C.I. so much as asks to speak to Baron, his dad'll have the top lawyer in the country at his side in ten seconds."

Of course, Baron had the right to get a lawyer whenever he so chose. But whether Baron was innocent or guilty, it was a lot harder getting answers out of a lawyer than out of the lawyer's client.

"Oh. That's a good point. I'll give them the head's up."

"Thank you," I hissed under my breath and returned to my computer. With Lehman, there was no such thing as a simple conversation.

While he put in the call, I returned to my databases. My next stop was NCIC, or the National Crime Information Center, a phenomenal black hole of criminal information maintained by the FBI. I plugged Baron's name, driver's license, and license plate into every search I could think of: Criminal history, negative. Past arrests, negative. Warrants, negative. I finally tried a QQ—also known as a Query Query and the ultimate proof that cop speak is redundant. With the QQ, I could see the last search *someone else* had made on Baron and where that cop or investigator was from. Maybe Baron had been pulled over for a traffic violation and some beat cop had run his license plate.

But even the QQ turned up a negative.

"Damn it," I muttered. Had he never so much as run out a parking meter?

I didn't notice Lehman hovering behind my chair until he slurped noisily out of the giant coffee mug he carried around the office. *Top Cop,* it said. I took umbrage with that mug.

"You realize D.C.I. will take care of all that?" he said, waving the mug at my screen.

"I'm curious, that's all."

"Well, just don't let curiosity kill the cop. There's a reason we handed this case over."

"If I find anything interesting, I'll turn it over to D.C.I."

Lehman shrugged. "Okay, I guess you're a big girl now. Oh, that reminds me, I got you a present." He snagged a rectangular box off the corner of his desk and plopped it onto the corner of mine. No bigger than his hand, it was wrapped in paper featuring a dozen varieties of fish.

I glanced between it and him. "What is this?"

"Open it."

I did. Inside the box was a foam fish, colored like a   - rainbow trout. Printed along the side were the words *Gone Fishin'.*

"It's a stress ball," Lehman explained. "Only it's a fish."

Eyes glazed, I stared at him. "Seriously?"

"Now you don't need your Glock."

I balled up the fish and threw it at the middle of his chest. Snickering, he beat a hasty retreat to his own desk. I left the fish abandoned in the middle of the floor and focused my attention once again on my screen. Out for blood now for any scrap of info I could find on Baron Hackett, I turned to Facebook and Twitter, then remembered to check this thing that was getting popular with teens, Instagram.

Baron's Facebook profile was shut up tight. I couldn't see anything beyond his profile picture and header image without friending him. Made sense. It sounded like the Hackett family had had problems with both the paparazzi and rabid fans in Hollywood. Baron apparently took his and his sister's security seriously.

His Twitter feed was almost as sparse. Maybe twice a month, he retweeted people like Elon Musk, Warren Buffet, and Tony Robbins. On occasion, he linked to various newspaper articles. On closer inspection, they were all about his family members. His dad's bid for office in Walworth County. His sister winning an acting award. His father backing a zero-waste factory in Iowa. One article from the local paper showed how Baron himself was spearheading an effort by local teens to keep blue-green algae blooms from appearing on Geneva Lake. Another article from his days in California showed him as the spokesperson for a teen mission to help homeless youth in LA.

I clicked through to the website of the Lake Geneva Regional News and placed a search for Baron's name. During a ceremony at the high school last spring, Baron had won no fewer than three awards.

I frowned at my screen. This couldn't be the same kid who'd broken into our police station.

"Hello, hello, hello!" A cheerful voice broke the silence as a uniformed officer walked into the detective bureau, a cardboard box under his arm. Thirty-something, hair cropped military-style, he had the easy-going manner of a man whose job it was to be cool in the eyes of fifteen hundred teenagers. For nine months out of the year, Mark Neumiller was our school resource officer at Badger High, where he had an office. In the summer, when Lake Geneva could swell to three times its normal size, Neumiller served as a third detective in our bureau.

Lehman's chair groaned as he leaned back. "My God, they let you out of school? You passed your final exams?"

Neumiller grinned and pinched his fingers together. "Scraped by, just barely." He set the box on a third desk against the wall, shoving aside stacks of paper and a model of a red-hot Porsche. "Dude, seriously what is all this?"

Lehman waved casually at the clutter. "I'm utilizing departmental resources. You're not even at that desk for nine months out of the year."

"Okay, okay, I get it. But this spot is mine now, so shove this shit somewhere else."

Lehman groaned and got out of his chair, then began to stack the paperwork on his own desk.

Neumiller nodded across the room as he unpacked his cardboard box. "Steele, how's it going?"

I leaned around my cubicle wall, eyes narrowed. "Do you know Baron Hackett?"

Neumiller placed a family photo next to his computer monitor. "Baron? Sure. Everybody knows him. Why?"

"We just got an anonymous tip that he might be involved in our break-in."

Neumiller pulled a skeptical frown. "Probably some jealous classmate trying to take him down a peg. Baron's a straight-A student. Team quarterback. National Honor Society. He was school treasurer this year. Next year, he's running for president." Neumiller shrugged. "He's a good kid, you know? Everybody loves him."

I frowned and chewed a hangnail. This wasn't adding up. The girl I'd just talked to over the phone was almost too nervous to talk. Then again, she would be, if she was turning in the most popular boy in school. If personal experience had taught me anything, it was that people could change radically, even when you thought you knew them as well as your own soul. It was hard to believe sometimes that the man I'd married was the same asshole I'd eventually divorced.

Still, I was faced with two versions of Baron Hackett. Was one real, the other fake? If so... which one?

CHAPTER TEN
BAILEY

I slipped out of the bathroom and ran back up the main deck.

"There she is!" yelled Noah, a boy in my grade with blond hair and a smile that was way too confident and friendly for my comfort level. This was his first time trying out, too. "Bai-*ley*! Bai-*ley*!" He chanted and clapped his hands. The other kids joined in.

Oh, God, I was gonna die. I ducked my head and hurried past them, but couldn't take my eyes off Baron. He was still sideways in his chair, for all the world as if nothing earth-shattering had just happened. Nothing that would maybe alter the course of his life forever. He just gave me a grin and a nod, as if saying *You got this.*

My face felt numb and cold. I had to focus. *I never called the police station,* I told myself, as if it were true. *This is the day you've been waiting for—mail jumping. This is a really, really good day.* I tore my eyes from Baron and scuttled to the front of the boat. Tommy stood at the helm, guiding us in a lazy circle so I could run at the same pier everyone else had.

He cocked half a grin. "You ready?"

I bobbed my head—again, as if it were true. But I couldn't feel my extremities. Probably a bad thing for mail jumping.

Melissa held up my mock delivery, a bunch of envelopes rolled up inside a newspaper. A rubber band held the entire bundle together. She placed it firmly in my upturned hand. Thus bestowed with the scepter of the office I hoped to occupy, I scooted to the large square window at Tommy's right. As high as my hip, it sat wide open, the glass insert stowed against the wall on the opposite side of the boat.

I threw one leg over the sill. My outside foot found the rub board. My inside foot found the bracket bolted to the floor, like an upside-down stirrup. It had been specially mounted to help the mail jumpers keep steady. The wind whipped my hair and spit a fine mist into my face, some from the sky, some from the waves breaking under the bow. Under the rub board, the water rolled dark blue and foamy white. The shoreline and the piers whipped by.

Oh my God, I was sitting in the mail jumper's window. I hadn't expected it to feel so… exhilarating. Like a mermaid riding a charging seahorse. The Mailboat's engines rumbled through my bones. A grin spread across my lips as my whole body unexpectedly relaxed. This felt sooo good. So right. Like I'd been born for this. Like the Mailboat was part of me. Like the spirit of its wooden body ran through my veins.

Tommy pushed the two levers beside his helm. If he was slowing the boat down, I couldn't tell. The pier felt like it was speeding toward us. "Use as much runway as you need," Tommy said.

Instead of sticking straight out into the lake, this pier ran parallel to the shore, creating a slip for the owner's boat. In the middle of this runway was the mailbox. Fixed to the top of a pier post, it stared me down. I mean, literally. The box was shaped like a badger, a wooden craft-fair find painted black, white, and gray. Its little black feet hugged the mailbox and a dark shiny eye locked gazes with me.

Gripping the handrail above my head, I pulled my other leg through the window. I was standing on the rub board now, the lake flying beneath my feet. I held the mail in an iron grasp so there was no chance of it getting away.

Back in the boat, the kids clapped and cheered. "Go, Bailey! You can do it!"

"Just keep your eye on the pier," Tommy coached as it charged closer, a javelin waiting to unseat me.

"And don't forget to kiss the badger!" Melissa called.

Kiss the badger? Oh, yeah. It was a tradition. All the mail jumpers kissed the badger...

The first pier post swung by.

"There you go, right there." Was it just me, or was Tommy's voice tense? Why would *he* be nervous?

There was no time to think about it. I launched myself off the side of the boat. My feet hit the pier, but my body kept running as if the Mailboat had flung me away, a dog shaking water out of its fur. Momentum. Account for momentum! Isn't that what Baron had told me?

I'd run clear past the badger before I knew it, but it was okay. It was a long pier. I'd just reel myself in before I sailed clean off the end.

That's when my shoe slipped out from under me, the rainwater offering zero traction. My right hip crashed to the deck. Then just like a Slip n' Slide, I careened across the pier... over the white-painted boards... off the edge.

My yelp was choked off by lake water and cascades of bubbles.

CHAPTER ELEVEN
TOMMY

"Oh-h-h-h-h!" the kids chorused and rushed to the windows.

Melissa sighed, shaking her head. "She didn't kiss the badger."

I didn't answer. My breath was caught in my throat. I kept one eye on the path of the boat, another on the place where Bailey had gone in. I didn't breathe again until Bailey surfaced. She came up like a fish catching flies, opening her mouth wide for air. A cheer rose from the other candidates as she doggy-paddled the few strokes to the ladder on the side of the pier.

She looked okay, thank goodness. That was a hard fall. I had no doubt she'd bear the battle wounds for a while. But the longer-lasting damage might be to her score. I glanced at the judges. They whispered to one another, shaking their heads, clicking their tongues, marking their clip boards.

I sighed. It was mail jumper tryouts. You were practically guaranteed a few kids would end up in the lake.

I'd just hoped it wouldn't be Bailey.

CHAPTER TWELVE
BAILEY

In the end, I guess one splash into the lake wasn't the worst thing ever. Anyway, Celeste Jones fell in twice and forgot to grab outgoing mail once, so I had to be light years ahead of her.

She and I huddled on the Riviera Pier in a pair of beach towels one of the judges had been generous enough to bring along. The judges were still on the boat, their chairs huddled close on the main deck as they compared notes. Within moments, we would all know our fates.

"Well, I know *I'm* stocking potato chips this summer," Celeste said, teeth chattering. While we'd dried off some, it was still overcast and we hadn't warmed up at all. The drizzle clung to Celeste's tight, curly black hair like pearls and dripped gently on her terry cape.

I shrugged. "But your reading was really good." And it was. Standing instead of sitting, she had barely glanced at the script, even though she was new to it, and projected so clearly she wouldn't have needed the microphone. She even smiled at the audience—the judges, jumpers, and reporters. She seemed to know all the right places to pause, to talk a little softer, to talk a little louder. It was like a night at the theater, and I knew my own reading had been mud by comparison.

"Yeah, maybe I should stick to speech club," she said. "'Cause dang, I ain't no mermaid out on those piers!" She laughed, even slapped her knee. Her teeth flashed white against her warm brown skin.

I wished I could be as nonchalant. I had peeked once during my reading, and there had been nothing but eyes, real and electronic, all staring at me. My heart had pounded out of my chest. *Why are you all staring at me? What have I done wrong?* I wanted to ask. *Is it because I fell in? Because I reported Baron?* And my brain nearly tailspinned into a panic attack.

And then I'd caught a glimpse of Tommy out of the corner of my eye. He was steering us back to home port, staring over the lake, mouthing the script along with me, the way a parent does when their six-year-old is in the school Christmas pageant.

It was super tacky, and yet it worked. I remembered to sit up straight. To breathe slowly. I tried looking at the audience again, and it wasn't so scary. They looked like they were actually listening or something—which was the weirdest experience of my life. Maybe I was doing okay? Anyway, the next time I glanced at Tommy, the corner of his mouth was lifted in a tiny smile. The judges seemed to grin as well as they marked up their clip boards. Maybe there was hope?

Baron's reading had been last. He wasn't as flamboyant as Celeste, but he spoke in an even tone and didn't pick up the book at all. He had it memorized. As such, he was able to join eyes with the audience the entire time. He wasn't being a show-off, either. It was like he was just having a conversation. I was so scared he might look at *me* that I stared at my hands the whole time, crunched tight inside my fuzzy towel.

A stirring on the pier jolted me out of my mental performance review. Everyone was staring at the windows along the boat. Inside, the judges nodded all around, smiling at each other, and tucked their clip boards under their arms. They rose from their chairs. My heart hammered in my chest. Did I talk too fast during my reading? Did I skip lines? Did I forget to put the flag down on a mailbox? Did I fall off more piers than I remembered? It wouldn't be the first time I'd blanked out bad memories.

The judges filed down the gangplank. The cameras started rolling again. Our boss, Robb Landis, stood in the middle of the pier and rubbed his hands together. He wore a fairly normal-looking black rain jacket, but also a pair of salmon pink chino shorts and hemp-braided flip-flops. His lakeside fashion was perfectly on point at all times and at the same time vaguely eccentric. "All right! Ladies and gentlemen, we have our results. First of all, thank you, candidates, for trying out today. You all put in your best, and it showed. It was a hard decision in the end."

But was it? Some of us had clearly done worse than others. I glanced between Celeste's terry towel and my own, then, as if seeking some kind of reassurance, I looked to Captain Tommy. Standing at the bow, he calmly uncoiled a huge electrical cable and plugged it into the port on the boat to recharge its massive batteries. Then he brushed his palms together and turned to watch. Like me, like all of us, he kept his eyes on Robb Landis.

"Okay," Robb said. "First up..." He glanced at the list one of the judges held and drummed his hands on a pier post, letting the sound rise to a crescendo. "Baron Hackett!"

In a show of solidarity, the kids burst into applause. The people working the cameras zoomed in for a shot of Baron's grinning face.

"Step on up here, Baron!" Robb motioned to the rub board on the side of the Mailboat. Baron quietly stepped into his assigned position, clasped one wrist in the opposite hand, and allowed another smile for the cameras. I imagined grace like that had been carefully cultivated in the environment of Baron's high-flying family. I knew if my name was called, I'd be smiling like an idiot.

"Our next mail jumper is... Melissa Kraft!"

Melissa smoothed a strand of brown-blond hair out of her face and stood on the rub board next to Baron.

"Mail jumper number three... Noah Cadigan!"

"Woo!" Noah pumped a fist and ran toward the Mailboat. Half-way across the pier, he did a cartwheel. Everybody laughed, and Noah hopped onto the rub board, smiling from ear-to-ear. Yep. That would be like me. Only if I tried a cartwheel I'd end up in the lake again.

Three spots filled. Only three to go. I bit my lips together.

Robb called out two more names. "Lacie Mulhullan!... Myles Trainer!"

One more slot. I closed my eyes. Please, God. I'd never ask for anything ever again. Just let me be a mail jumper...

"Okay," Rob said, "one more mail jumper will make the 2013 team. I just want to say again what a great job you all did. We're so proud of you and so happy you wanted to be on the team. Those of you not making it this year, we really do hope you'll try again next year. Okay, with that said, here's our final mail jumper."

My eyes were still closed. My jaw locked together. *Just this once, let something good happen.*

"Alisha McCormick!"

Alisha screamed and jogged to the Mailboat, joining the rest of the team on the rub board.

My heart broke cleanly in two, as if water had been pooling and freezing, forming a crack there all along. I hadn't made it.

I hadn't made it.

Robb spread out an arm toward the six kids standing on the side of the Mailboat. "Judges, ladies and gentlemen of the press, may I present the 2013 Lake Geneva mail jumpers!"

Cameras flashed and guys with recorders over their shoulders panned down the line of victors.

"Tommy, get over here." Robb waved. "They need a shot of the captain with his crew."

Tommy shook his head as if all the hoopla were a little ridiculous, but he obliged, stepping slowly up onto the rub board at the head of the line. More flashes. More minutes of footage. More smiling faces.

I would have given everything I owned to be standing where Baron stood, right beside the captain. Why did everybody else get wonderful things in life? Why did I always end up with the short straw? I fought back tears. I didn't want the camera crews or my boss to think I was a spoiled brat and having a fit.

I just...

I didn't want to be a foster kid anymore.

I didn't want to be alone anymore.

"You know, I'm kinda glad I didn't get the job," Celeste whispered in my ear. "I figured out last-minute I ain't got the nerve."

I tuned her out. I didn't have the nerve, either, and yet I was willing to find it, if only I could be a mail jumper.

But I wasn't.

CHAPTER THIRTEEN
TOMMY

A smile pasted onto my face for the benefit of the weekly paper, I tried to see past the flashing cameras. Tried to see Bailey. How was she taking it?

I finally spotted her beyond the throng of reporters. A striped blue and white towel clasped around her shoulders, she stared blankly at the new team. The single tear that slipped down her cheek told me all I needed to know. She'd worked hard for this. And her spot had been given to somebody else.

I wanted to tell her that it was okay. That she'd done well. That she could try again next year. But a year in the life of a teenager was, of course, forever. So I tried to think what else I could say. My mind drew a blank—other than to demand of myself why I cared at all.

I'd seen countless candidates turned away. Some eventually made the team. Others never tried again. The waves washed ashore whatever they may. It wasn't my place to care.

And yet I did. Maybe I was just a selfish old man, wanting to keep close to me the one person who could tempt a little joy from my dry and weathered soul, like sap running anew in long-dead driftwood. Maybe even I still wanted to dream now and again.

CHAPTER FOURTEEN
BARON

Baron rolled down the winding, oak-lined drive to the house on the South Shore. A boxy, modernist mansion painted dark taupe, the architect had broken up its patterned lines by off-setting the picture windows. From the inside, the vast sheets of glass practically brought the lake and the woods indoors, mixing nature with minimalism. It wasn't a bad place to call home.

Tonight, two extra cars sat in front of the garage. Apparently the Hacketts had company. Not unusual. On any given day of the week, Baron's mom might have friends over or his dad might have brought home a business associate.

Baron pulled up beside the extra cars and killed the engine. Then he sat staring at the blue and white BMW emblem in the middle of the steering wheel.

Today was hard.

After tryouts, he'd worked a full-lake tour on one of the paddle wheel boats. The slow sojourn around the lake had mostly provided a chance to dwell on the last few days. The stress simmering just below the surface. The exhaustion it brought on. But it wasn't in a Hackett's nature to be tired.

Work twice as hard as the competition. That's what his parents had taught both him and his sister. It was their ethic. It's what had won Baron a spot on the mail jumping team and everything else he'd accomplished in life.

But he was sorry Bailey hadn't made the team, too. She had been nervous and it had interfered with her performance. But a single fall into the lake wasn't grounds for disqualification. Other candidates had simply been better.

Well, in good news, she might still have a chance. Depending on what fate had in store for Baron. Each second of the clock felt like a bomb ticking down toward an inevitable detonation. The only question was how many seconds were left. A million? A thousand? Ten? It depended whether Bailey had ever reported him. Some of the kids at school thought she was stupid because she was quiet. But they were wrong. She was an observer. She took in everything around her. The question was whether she ever let the things she knew back into the world again.

He grabbed his backpack, got out of the car, and mounted the beige-painted porch to the front door. As he walked into the living room with its vaulted ceiling and dark hardwood floors, the smell of steaks and sizzling onions greeted him, and with it laughter and conversation. Baron kicked off his shoes and walked around the massive, double-sided fireplace into the kitchen.

"There's our Baron!" exclaimed his mother's cousin, holding her arms out wide.

"Hey, Deb," Baron said, stepping into the hug. When she released him, her husband Jerry gave him a friendly slap on the shoulder. Baron exchanged nods with their son Chad, who sat at the black marble island with a beer. Baron's sister Regina sat next to him, dunking crackers in jalapeno dip.

"How were tryouts?" Baron's mom asked. Tonya Hackett stood behind the stove in the middle of the island, a petite woman with messy brown hair stuck through with chopsticks. Silver bangles glinted on her wrists and around her neck.

Baron joined her behind the stove and leaned in to give her a kiss. "Great. Made the team again."

The family erupted into cheers. While the Hacketts held high standards, they also offered high praise. It wasn't a bad arrangement.

"Nice job, Baron." His mom's smug smile said she'd known all along he wouldn't fail.

"Will we see you on the news tonight?" Baron's father, Richard Hackett, was still wearing his business suit but held a glass of wine in one hand.

"They gave me an interview at the end," Baron replied.

Richard checked his watch. "We'll be sure to turn on the TV at six."

Baron smiled, but a little sadly. For the first time, he didn't deserve the accolades. The clock was ticking down. The things he had done would catch up to him. He wouldn't be on the team long enough to have earned the celebration. But none of his family knew that. Not yet.

Tonya turned to her cousin Deb's son. "But back to what we were talking about, Chad. This incident isn't going to be counted against your probation, is it? Will this affect your ability to be confirmed on the police department?"

Chad Rauch stared at his beer bottle. "God, I hope not. I only just got signed off by my field training officer."

Baron slid a Ritz cracker off his sister's plate and dipped it in the creamy white sauce. "What happened?"

Instead of answering, Chad continued to stare at his beer, his face turning warm pink.

Regina offered the explanation for him. "His key to the police station went missing."

Chad sighed through puffed cheeks. "No, it was stolen. It had to have been. I just can't think how. Then somebody used it to break into the PD and attacked one of the telecommunicators..." He raked his hands through his hair. "I've been wracking my brains, thinking over every contact I made with the public that day. I just can't think how it could have... Did I drop it?"

Baron looked Chad in the eye. "I'm really sorry, man."

Chad merely leaned his chin in his palm and shook his head. Of course, he had no way of knowing what Baron really meant. He was sorry for lifting the key card and putting Chad into this position. Such a simple thing, to slip it out of his jacket pocket two nights ago. And yet the regret sat in Baron's soul like a well, the bottom so far from the surface that the water swirled inky black. But Baron had already laid a thick layer of ice over the top. He couldn't afford to get hung up by the profoundness of his regret. Chad had no idea the depths of the game Baron was navigating. There had been no other way... Chad would understand. One day. A long, long time from now.

Tonya reached across the counter and patted Chad's arm. "It'll be fine. You made a mistake, but this doesn't have to be the end."

Chad nodded miserably. "It's just hard."

"Harder makes you stronger," Richard said.

Chad flashed him a smile, then forced himself to sit up a little taller. "Yes, sir."

Richard lifted his wine glass toward him. "Atta boy. You've got this."

Harder makes you stronger. Another Hackett family mantra. Baron held it in his mind. He'd need it to help him endure the road ahead.

Tonya scraped her caramelized onions over a platter of steaks, steaming and stewing in juices. "Let's not dwell on it. New topic. Deb, you have no idea how much we owe you for recommending Lake Geneva when we decided to leave LA. Reggie just needed someplace quiet to focus on school until graduation..."

Baron's mom and her cousin chattered on about Lake Geneva and everything it had to offer—not least of which, more privacy for the Hackett family. A privacy Baron was about to ruin again. He studied his parents' happy faces. They would understand. They would see why he did what he did. They would support him, like always.

Just as they were trooping to the dinner table with serving dishes piled high, the phone rang in its cradle on the kitchen counter.

"I'll get it," Baron said. He put down the salad and picked up the phone as the rest of the family moved into the dining room. "Hello?"

A female voice replied. "Hello. May I speak with Baron Hackett, please?"

He didn't recognize the voice, and yet something cold twisted in his stomach. In his soul, he knew this was it. The clock had ticked down to zero. But he would have turned himself in anyway if the wait had dragged on too long. "This is Baron," he replied.

"My name is Special Agent Emory Mullins," the woman went on. "I'm with the Wisconsin Department of Criminal Investigations. I was told you might have some information that could help with a case I'm working on."

She was told he had information? Not that he was a suspect? An interesting angle—one Baron hadn't anticipated. But in a heartbeat, he adjusted to the tactic. It made sense. They wanted information. They assumed he would be reluctant to give it to them, and thus they would "lure" him in by suggesting he was only a witness and not a suspect.

On one point, they had miscalculated. He was more than ready to give them information.

"How can I help you?" Baron asked.

"Would you be willing to meet me at the Lake Geneva Police Department for an interview?"

"Yes. When?"

"I can meet you in an hour."

Baron checked the clock on the kitchen wall—a sheet of glass with silver hands, no numerals. It was five P.M. Agent Mullins was working overtime and they wanted him in fast. Because they were that sure he was their man? Because they knew his dad's lawyer could make the drive from Chicago in ninety minutes?

"I'll be there," Baron replied. And the lawyer wouldn't. The man would have a heart attack if he knew what Baron was about to do.

"Great," the woman said. "Just tell them at the PD lobby that you're there to meet Agent Mullins. They'll show you where to go."

"Will do."

"Thank you. See you in an hour."

"See you in an hour." And then the wait would be over. The anxiety in his chest could be released.

Baron hung up. He inhaled slowly and let it all out, then followed his family into the dining area.

"Did you bring the salad, honey?" his mom asked.

Instead of answering, Baron looked at her and his father. "Mom, Dad, can I talk to you? Privately?"

"Of course." His dad set down the water pitcher with which he'd been filling glasses. "What is it?"

Baron met his parents' gazes steadily. "I've gotta tell you something."

CHAPTER FIFTEEN
MONICA

I plugged a key into a metal plate mounted to the wall outside the interview room door. "You know how these work," I said to Agent Emory Mullins. "Just turn to the right and the video will start recording."

"Got it." Mullins' auburn hair was trimmed in a practical boy cut. She wore a navy two-piece suit and no jewelry. Minimal makeup—just a touch of mascara. She was all business. I liked her. I pulled the key from the switch and handed it to Mullins, who put it in her pocket.

We stood in the middle of the secured waiting room, a cluster of chairs sitting by racks of literature—help for domestic violence, self-defense classes, McGruff the Crime Dog. "Coffee and water are through that door in the break room," I went on. "Give the door a tug and Angie will let you through." Like all the doors in the station, the telecommunicators had control via a switch panel at their desk. "Vending machine's right here, if he wants a snack."

"Sounds good."

I glanced up and down the waiting room and tapped my foot, wondering if I was forgetting anything. Any minute, Baron Hackett would walk through the door.

Nerves raced up and down my spine. Finally, I'd know what kind of kid he was: a model young citizen, or a petty criminal who broke into locked buildings and attacked anyone who got in his way. Hopefully, I'd also find out whether he was working for Sergeant Horace Stubbs. I could feel the truth churning in my gut. Stubbs wanted those records destroyed. He'd found the most unlikely kid to do it. He'd crafted what he thought was the perfect crime. My fists clenched and loosened at the thought of finally seeing the man behind bars where he belonged.

"Anything else you need?" I asked.

Agent Mullins shook her head. "I think that'll do. Thanks for letting me use your facility."

I shrugged. "Any time." In fact, I was delighted. This was officially Mullins' case, not mine due to that conflict of interest problem. I wouldn't have any part in the interview or in following up with clues that may be revealed. But at least I'd be close to the action.

The door from the lobby buzzed open and a young man walked through. I stood a little straighter, nostrils flaring, a dog on alert. This was him, I knew it. Baron Hackett. My eyes scanned up and down, mining for clues. He was tall. Muscular. Of course. Quarterback. For the occasion, he'd dressed casual yet smart: khaki shorts and a striped polo shirt, royal blue and white. His dark hair was styled in a carefree, windblown look. A diamond stud glittered in one ear and a cowrie shell necklace hung around his neck. He looked every bit the accomplished yet popular boy all of Badger High was in love with.

"Hello," he said, shoulders square, his presentation completely on-point. "I'm looking for Agent Mullins."

"That's me." Mullins shook his hand. "Thanks for coming in. Is there anything I can get you before we start? Water? Coffee? Need anything to eat?"

Baron shook his head. "I'm good, thank you. I'm ready whenever you are."

"Perfect." Mullins nodded toward the interview room. "C'mon in and make yourself at home."

Baron strode through the door. Before following him in, Mullins plugged the key I'd given her into the switch and turned it to the right. Then she stepped into the room and closed the door behind her.

I spun on my heel, hip-checked the lock on the door to the break room, and made for the stairwell; the elevator was too slow for my patience levels. I took the steps two at a time and coursed down the hall to the detective bureau. At my own desk, I threw myself into my chair and grabbed for my computer mouse. Something soft and squishy filled my hand instead—the foam stress trout Lehman had given me. I batted it aside and found my mouse a few inches away. I woke up my computer. The video software was already open on my screen. I parked a set of headphones over my ears and hit play. After a second of blackness, the screen filled with a bird's-eye view of the interview room downstairs.

Baron Hackett sat on one side of the gray, Formica-topped table, the camera pointed toward his face. Agent Mullins sat opposite him.

"Address?" Mullins was saying, her hand moving across a notebook on the table in front of her. She was still gathering the basics. Baron provided the answers one-by-one as she requested them. When she was done, she leaned back in her chair. "Thanks, Baron." She crossed her legs and laced her fingers around her knee, by all appearances ready to start the interview proper.

But Baron spoke up first. "I think you're looking for this." He reached into a cargo pocket on his shorts and laid something small, white, and rectangular on the table.

A key card.

I sat upright in my chair, pulse racing.

Mullins stared at the key card, lips parted. She was off her game. I could see it. Baron was in here based off an anonymous tip—a junk tip, as the majority of them were. She hadn't anticipated a confession. And first thing in the interview? Unheard of.

But she only froze for a beat before switching gears smoothly. "Can you explain where you got that?"

"My second cousin, Chad Rauch, is an officer with the Lake Geneva Police Department," Baron replied. "I took it from his jacket pocket on June 9th, two days ago. Then I used it to break into the police station that same night."

I shifted an eyebrow at him. *You cocky bastard.* So that was Baron's type: the attention whore. Winning awards wasn't good enough for him. He wanted renown, for good deeds or evil. He wanted the world to know what he'd done. What he was capable of.

I leaned back and tapped a finger on my chin. So our hapless rookie, Chad Rauch, was Baron Hackett's cousin. Correction: second cousin. That's how I'd missed the connection despite all my research. I hadn't thought to look up distantly related family. I snarled to myself. Stupid oversight. I'd do better next time.

To her credit, Mullins was now taking everything in stride. She didn't so much as unlace her fingers. "Baron, it's my duty to inform you that you are now under arrest."

"I understand," he replied.

"You have the right to remain silent..." she proceeded with the rest of the Miranda warning.

I clasped my hands in front of my mouth like an eager, finger-biting prayer. This was it. We'd gotten him. The person who had attacked Steph Buchanan. Steph and her family would be relieved. The entire police department could relax. We'd avenged our pack member. Sent another low-life piece of shit to jail. I wished I knew who had called in with that anonymous tip. This one had been golden. Nail on the head. I'd like to personally thank the girl. But I'd probably never know who it was.

"Do you understand these rights as I have explained them to you?" Mullins concluded.

"I do."

"Do you waive the right to have an attorney present during questioning?"

"Yes. And I'd like the chance to speak freely before you proceed with your own questions."

Mullins waved a hand. "Go ahead." She'd be an idiot to turn him down. He was on a roll and there was no bean he wouldn't spill.

But I frowned. Something was wrong. He was so... *polite*. There was no pride. No boasting. He wasn't acting like an attention junkie. He could be on the Autism spectrum, but I wasn't convinced of that yet. What was this, then? A need to unload? But that didn't feel right, either. I stared intently into Baron's face, desperate to understand. His features remained calm, smooth. He could have been taking an interview regarding a job for which he knew he was well-qualified. I leaned an elbow on my knee and chewed a nail. He was one up on me. I hated this.

"First, I apologize for any wrongs I've done," Baron proceeded, "and any harm I may have caused. I needed a particular set of records. Records pertaining to a former LGPD officer, Sergeant Horace Stubbs."

This was it, the part where Baron admitted he was working for Stubbs. That Stubbs was desperate to clean up a dirty past. To not only lock Roger Holland up but to throw away the key. I tasted sweet victory. I fixed my eyes on Baron Hackett and waited for it.

"My only goal was to prove the innocence of a man who has been serving time for a murder he never committed. Roger Holland."

My jaw fell loose. Wait, what? As I sat gaping, the leg-up Baron had on me expanded into a decisive lead and I was eating his dust.

"Please explain," Mullins said.

"On August 29, 1995, Roger Holland was arrested for supposedly murdering his friend, Kent Bullinger. The arresting officer was Sergeant Horace Stubbs. But another officer present that day, Officer Monica Steele, filed a written complaint against Stubbs, suggesting that he had altered crime scene evidence to make the death appear as a murder, not an accident. No one ever followed up on Officer Steele's complaint. Holland went to trial for murder and was convicted and has been behind bars ever since."

I stared at Baron Hackett. What was happening?

Mullins tapped her pen on her notepad. "Do you realize you're raising very serious allegations against an officer of the law?"

Instead of answering, Hackett pulled a paper from his pocket and unfolded it on the table. "Here's a copy of the complaint that was filed by Officer Steele. Until now, I believe no one ever laid eyes on it, besides Steele and her lieutenant at the time, Theodore Townsend. On the morning of June 10th, I mailed the original to Roger Holland's attorney. My guess is that he'll use it to demand a retrial."

I stared at the screen, my mind and my emotions a total blank. This wasn't about Stubbs covering his ass. It wasn't about Baron being the hired grunt. Baron was—

Baron was me. The over-achiever. The whistle-blower. The one small voice bent on seeing real justice done, whatever the cost. I couldn't approve of his methods. I never would. And yet in a weird way, we were on the same side. It twisted my soul into a pretzel to try to wrap my mind around it.

I bowed my head over my desk and massaged my temples. Well, this was why we'd handed the case over to D.C.I. Completely drunk on bias and revenge, I'd refused to consider other possibilities. Damn idiot.

Mullins leaned forward and glanced over the report. "How did you know this document even existed?"

"I work with Roger Holland's granddaughter, Melissa Kraft. The family has always maintained that Roger was innocent. That he'd never kill his best friend. Melissa's mother claims that at the time of Roger Holland's trial, Officer Steele implied that the trial was somehow unlawful. That another officer was to blame."

I closed my eyes and groaned. I'd forgotten all about that. I'd been furious that the case had been allowed to proceed to trial. In a moment of unscrupulous rage, I'd let something slip. *It's not your dad's fault; it's Stubbs'.* Something to that effect. No doubt it had given the family hope. But of course, they'd never had any evidence. None of us had.

Mullins picked the document up and read it more carefully, the report I had crafted so passionately as a young cop. The one that had branded me as an idiot back in the day. When she was finished, she turned to Baron once again. "So you broke into the Lake Geneva Police Department to steal this written complaint. You did it to try to exonerate a prisoner. Did you also attack a police department employee who arrived on the scene to investigate your break-in?"

Baron flexed his jaw. His eyes saddened, yet refused to look away from Agent Mullins. "It was an accident. I had what I'd come for. I was leaving. Then I saw the woman in the hallway. I stopped to decide what to do. But I bumped a board that was leaning against a wall. It hit her on the back of the head. I made sure she was breathing comfortably, then I left the building. I never meant to hurt anyone."

Mullins looked at him dubiously. "Why, Baron? Why break into a police station? Why take the risk? The risk of being intercepted, the risk of being caught. You didn't even know Roger Holland." She glanced over her notes. "You weren't even born at the time of his incarceration."

I knew his answer before he spoke it. I knew it because I'd said the exact same thing to my then-husband. *Why are you doing this, Monica?* he had pleaded with me. We'd only just bought the picture frames for the snapshots of us being sworn into office. He knew as well as I did that blowing the whistle on my superior, a man who had the favor of his own superior, could spell the end of my fledgling career. That was back when we'd actually cared about each other.

Baron put his finger on the paper between him and Agent Mullins. "This complaint has been sitting in the LGPD's storage room for eighteen years. At least one person still working for the department knew it was there. And yet she never did anything about it, even when the people who previously stood in her way were retired. For eighteen years, an innocent man has been in jail while the guilty one walks free." Baron stared deeply into Agent Mullins' eyes. "I did it because—"

I said it with him. "—no one else had the guts to do the right thing."

I closed my eyes and remembered the way my ex had looked at me. The understanding. The acceptance. The unspoken promise that he would stand by my side, no matter the blowback. And he had. Of course, that had been a lifetime ago, another world ago, and God only knew where he was now. Maybe rotting in hell, like I often hoped he was. But at the time, his support had meant everything to me.

I let Baron's accusations soak in. I was the one who'd let that piece of paper languish in storage while Holland languished in jail. I'd tried to raise Cain at first, but Lieutenant Townsend had hushed it all down. Laughed at "how little I knew." Implied I was a dumb female. That maybe I shouldn't wear the badge. Law enforcement was a man's world—more blatantly then than it was now. I'd gone from fighting for an innocent man to fighting for my own right to be on the police department.

Baron and Mullins' interview rolled on, as I knew it would for hours. I would listen to every minute, even though it felt like stabbing needles into my chest. I should have fought harder for Roger Holland. Instead, I'd unwittingly left it to a teenager to finish the work I'd abandoned, and to do it in a way that had harmed one of our own telecommunicators. It sickened me to admit it; I owed it to Baron Hackett for finally setting the record straight. Holland's. Stubbs'. My own.

He was going to prison for this. There was no question. He'd still broken into a police station, stolen police property, and injured a police department employee, intentionally or otherwise. Due to the seriousness of the offense, he might even be tried as an adult, which would carry with it stiffer penalties. Maybe the judge would show lenience, take into account Baron's motives and absence of any prior record. But the fact remained: he was giving up his freedom for someone else's. When Holland had first been arrested, I had acted all tough. But when the going got hard, I'd faltered. I utterly lacked Baron's kind of courage. When it came down to Holland's freedom or my badge, I'd chosen my badge.

My eyes filled with angry tears. Angry with myself. With my failure. My eye found the rainbow trout on the corner of my desk—*Gone Fishin'.* I grabbed it and flung it across the room.

WEDNESDAY
JUNE 12, 2013

CHAPTER SIXTEEN
BAILEY

I guess watching the same nature documentary three times in a row is pretty lame. But I was alone, like always. My foster dad was at his restaurant—he never quit working—and this was one of my favorite films ever. Penguins are so freaking adorable. And to be honest, I wasn't actually watching it. I was just trying not to cry. It was my day off, which meant there was nothing to distract me. To keep me from thinking. So I had banned myself from thinking. At all. About anything.

And that's how I found myself waddling up and down the snow-packed Antarctic, fluffing up my down and feeling utterly amazed that my webbed feet weren't even cold. Because I was a freaking penguin.

How close had I come to making the team? Like, really close? Not close at all? Did it matter? No. Because I *hadn't* made the team. An inch or a mile, it was all the same.

Oh, damn it, I was thinking. I stared hard at the penguins jumping off the sea ice like little tuxedoed torpedoes. I needed to be a penguin. There were anchovies out there. Lots of delicious, fat little anchovies...

My phone rang on the end table. I don't think I heard it the first two or three times. When I finally did, I had a panicked feeling—my non-penguin subconscious screaming at me—that there was only one ring left. I glanced at the screen. It said *Robb Landis*, my boss. Why would he be calling? I should probs pick it up. Like, before my phone sent him to voice mail.

"Hello?"

"Hey, Bailey, it's Robb. Say, we have a little problem. Turns out one of our mail jumpers... ah... Well, he won't be on the team this year."

"Oh, really?" My brain was still catching tiny silver fish somewhere off the coast of South America. Swarming in breathtaking synchronization with my fellow penguins. Wrapping that school of delicious little pizza toppers into an ever-tightening ball. Darting into their midst and filling my beak with squirming, life-giving meat.

I hate anchovies on pizza.

"Yeah," Robb babbled on. "So the judges and I had a quick meeting, and we've decided... Well, we'd like you to take the opening."

I picked off a squirming, oily little fish and swallowed it whole. I'd grab as many more as I could stuff into my belly, then swim back to the colony and puke it all up for the adorable little fluff-puffin squawking its tiny head off back at the nest.

Wait... What had Robb just said?

"You want... you want *me* to be on the mail jumping team?"

"That's right." Robb sounded like he was smiling. Like he enjoyed making someone's dearest wish come true. Like he was the guy who shows up at your front door with a check the size of a small marine research boat.

My brain was stuck halfway between Lake Geneva and the Antarctic. "Me?" I asked again, like I'd been swimming in ice-strewn waters too long and gotten a brain freeze.

Robb laughed. "Yes, Bailey. We'd like you to be on the mail jumping team this summer. Can you be at the Mailboat at seven Saturday morning?"

I finally realized I wasn't a penguin. *I was a mail jumper.* "Yes!" I squeaked, for all the world like a hungry fluff-puffin. "Yes, I'll be there!"

"Great! Thanks a million, Bailey. I'll shoot you an email with the rest of your schedule."

"Yes, sir. Thank you, sir."

He laughed. "Not a problem. Thanks for helping us out, Bailey."

We hung up.

I dropped my phone. It vanished somewhere into the depths of the lay-z-boy recliner. I clapped both hands over my mouth. Squeezed my eyes shut. Tried not to scream.

I was a mail jumper.

And then came the tears.

I was a mail jumper. I'd get to work with Tommy. Like, almost every day all summer long. Maybe for once I'd feel like I wasn't completely alone in the world. Maybe I'd feel like someone was actually there for me. Someone who got nervous for you when you were about to do something daring. Someone who helped you recite your lines when you had no idea what you were doing.

For once—finally—something good had happened in my life.

I got up from the chair, stretched my arms wide, and spun in circles. My belly happy and full of fish, I twirled all the way home through crystal-blue waters to the colony and a hungry little fluff-puffin.

SATURDAY
JUNE 15, 2013

CHAPTER SEVENTEEN
TOMMY

As I walked down the pier that Saturday morning, there was Bailey sitting on the bow of the Mailboat, feet dangling over the water, heels rocking back and forth. She had arrived even before me, and that was saying something.

I grinned. My last-minute mail jumper. Robb had called a couple nights ago with the change in plans. "That's fine," I'd said, heating up soup over the stove while Cubs vs. Reds played on the radio. "Tell her to wear something that dries fast."

He laughed. We hung up. I turned off the soup and leaned on the stovetop, staring at the backsplash and smiling like a damned old fool. Bailey-girl. She'd made the team. Ten minutes went by before I realized the ball game was over and the Cubs had lost. It didn't matter. Bailey was gonna be a mail jumper.

"Morning," I called as I got closer to the boat. She was dressed in navy shorts, a white tee shirt with the cruise line logo, and a pair of running shoes. Her ponytail hung over her shoulder and her fly-away hair haloed her face, almost honey-blond in the morning sun.

"Morning!" She jumped down from the boat, landed on the dock, and bounced on her toes, her hands clasped behind her back. Looking at her now, so young and eager and innocent as a new-born day, it was hard to believe what she'd done. She'd called the police and turned in Baron Hackett. I didn't know that from her or Robb or Chief Wade Erickson or anybody; I simply knew it. What else could explain Baron's absence, Bailey's presence, Robb's hushed admission that Baron had apparently gotten into some trouble with the law? As inconceivable as it was that Baron could be the guilty party, it was even more stunning to me that Bailey, my shy little clamshell, had been courageous enough to report him.

It would take a while to wrap my mind around the whole thing. But in the meantime, one fact was immutable: Bailey stuck her neck out to do the right, hard thing and ended up a mail jumper. While Baron's alleged crimes unsettled me on many levels, I guess I was okay with the outcome.

More than that. Something swelled in my chest like the lake before a storm. Pride. I hadn't felt that since my son had graduated college; gotten a solid job; swept his way up the corporate ladder to higher echelons of responsibility. I'd never told him how I felt. I wasn't sure I had the words to tell Bailey, either.

"What do you need me to do?" She grinned brightly, her cheeks flushed pink as if she'd run laps on the piers to burn off energy. She was clearly eager to begin her duties as a Lake Geneva mail jumper.

I hid my smile by bowing my head as I stuck my key in the lock. When I spoke, my voice adopted my old tone of a petty officer second class. "Grab some paper towels and wipe down these windows." I held the door open for her. "I want 'em all gleaming."

"Yes, sir!" Before I could remind her not to call me *sir*, she shot inside the boat and bee-lined for the cleaning closet in the aft.

I watched her go, shaking my head, then gazed over the lake. The water was azure blue and smooth as glass except where a family of ducks raised a few ripples below the boats. The sand grooming machine chugged along the nearby swimming beach, the operator whistling a little Frank Sinatra, one of my favorites, "That's Life." The trees along the shore were in full leaf, promising another glorious Lake Geneva summer full of laughter, cannon balls, and ice cream cones.

I sighed. This was going to be a good year.

I stepped into the boat to join my new mail jumper.

MONDAY
JUNE 17, 2013

CHAPTER EIGHTEEN
SKULL

Leaning against a tree, a narrow man in ratty black jeans and a hoodie watched the door of the Walworth County Judicial Center. With the sleeves ripped off his sweater, his tanned arms were bared to the sun, along with his favorite tattoo—the rose-schadel, a skull with a rose painted on its cracked white temple.

He checked his watch. The sentencing hearing couldn't take more than a few minutes. There had never even been a trial. No need. Baron had confessed to everything, leaving the judge nothing to do but decide how long to lock him up and how big a fine to leave for his rich-ass dad to pay.

The glass doors swung open and the man of the hour strode through. Baron Hackett walked tall and proud, dressed in a two-piece suit but flanked by sheriff's deputies. The boy's hands were cuffed behind his back. It was only a short stroll from here to the waiting squad car and a short ride from Walworth County to the juvenile detention facility in Racine.

As Baron and his guards passed, Skull tilted his head over a cigarette and lighter, letting his cupped hands and his hood conceal his face. Over his fingers, he glanced at the kid. They exchanged a look, nothing more. But in the brief moment their eyes met, Skull sent his thanks.

Their scheme had worked. The boy was taking the fall. Skull was going free. Baron hadn't done a thing besides lift his cousin's key card. Well, that and devise the alibi, the whole Stubbs-Holland angle. Genius bit of work, that was. *We've got to throw them a bone,* Baron had insisted. *Divert attention from what we're really after.* Lucky thing the kid had an inside scoop on that old, forgotten murder case. It was just the thing they'd needed. Skull had rifled the Stubbs-Holland papers while leaving the ones they were really after untouched. The original documents were safe and sound back at the police station, but their information locked away in Skull's brain.

Skull was free to move forward with the plan now. Meanwhile, Baron could assume all responsibility for the break-in while still looking like a bleeding saint. The incident with the police dispatcher had been an unlucky complication—Skull had seen no other way of escape but to crack her in the back of the head with one of the boards leaning against the wall. But Baron had managed to smooth even that one over, framing it as an accident. The kid was confident he wouldn't be behind bars long. He'd win the system over with his impeccable good behavior. Skull wasn't sure if the boy was brave or just stupid. Either way, Baron's sacrifice served his purposes.

And The Man's.

After all, it wasn't Skull whom Baron was trying to impress.

The sheriff's deputies tucked Baron away in the back seat, reminding him to watch his head. They got in the front. Closed the doors. Took off down the street in the direction of Racine.

Skull pulled his phone out of his pocket. He dialed a number he didn't keep in his contacts. A number he'd erase from his call history as soon as the conversation was over.

It rang once. The Man picked up. "Yes?"

Skull savored his anticipation. Took a drag from the cigarette. "It's all taken care of."

"You have the information?"

"Yep. You were right. The cops had a whole folder on the Markham Ring." Seventeen years ago, the Ring had gone down in a blaze of glory. Bobby Markham and his boys were caught red-handed in an alley behind the last bank they ever broke into, right in their home town of Lake Geneva. Bobby never lived to see the morrow.

"And?" The Man prodded.

Skull took another deep breath through the cigarette and blew a long column of smoke. "I know where to find Fritz." He let the words hang, knowing The Man's eagerness was coming into full blossom on the other end of the line. "The Plan can move forward."

JOIN THE CREW

———⊕———

Ahoy, Shipmate!

If you feel like you're perched on a lighthouse, scanning the horizon for Danielle Lincoln Hanna's next book—good news! You can subscribe to her email newsletter and read a regular ship's log of her writing progress. Better yet, dive deep into the life of the author, hear the scuttlebutt from her personal adventures, spy on her writing process, and catch a rare glimpse of dangerous sea monsters—better known as her pets, Fergus the cat and Angel the German Shepherd.

It's like a message in a bottle washed ashore. All you have to do is open it...

DanielleLincolnHanna.com/newsletter

BOOKS BY DANIELLE LINCOLN HANNA

The Mailboat Suspense Series

The Girl on the Boat: A prequel novella to the Mailboat
Suspense Series
Mailboat I: The End of the Pier
Mailboat II: The Silver Helm
Mailboat III: The Captain's Tale
Mailboat IV - *coming summer 2020*

DanielleLincolnHanna.com/shopnow

ACKNOWLEDGMENTS

Since I started writing the Mailboat Suspense Series, I've pictured snapshots of Bailey's life before she became a Lake Geneva mail jumper. Recently, I was inspired to capture one of those snapshots as a story (this one). In addition to exploring Bailey and Monica's lives, I was eager to reveal more of Tommy the way he was before the events of the main series took place. From Book One on, events unravel so quickly that I felt the reader never got a chance to see the relationship Bailey and Tommy had early on. I hope any curiosities have now been satisfied. As for Ryan... he's still a sergeant in Minneapolis, breaking womens' hearts and getting his tires slashed.

Even this short book wouldn't have been possible without the help of many friends. My thanks, as always, to the Lake Geneva Cruise Line (https://www.cruiselakegeneva.com/), operators of the real-life Lake Geneva Mailboat. Thank you for the inspiration. Gratitude specifically to *General Managers Harold Friestad (ret.)* and *Jack Lothian*, to *the Mailboat Captain Neill Frame*, and to *Office Manager Ellen Burling.*

I'm forever grateful to my expert advisers and the time they freely give to help me write better, more accurate stories. *Lieutenant Edward Gritzner, Sergeant Jason Hall,* and *Telecommunicator Rita Moore* of the Lake Geneva Police Department, thank you for explaining how an internal investigation would be handled, sharing tales of the old days when your dads and granddads were policing, and divulging that delicious detail about the "haunted doors" to the maintenance room. (Priceless.) *Sam Petitto (retired police officer),* thanks for your long emails brimming with information on crime databases and other topics that would bore most readers (but not me). *David Congdon* (Threat Assessment and Countermeasures Specialist), I can't express how much I appreciate our conversations on psychology and why on earth my characters do what they do.

To my long-time brainstorming partner, *Carrie Lynn Lewis*, thanks for helping me get unstuck on a particularly tricky detail. To my writer's club, *We Write Good*, thanks for being the first eyes on my manuscript and saving me from embarrassing myself with words I must have written while sleeping.

My dedicated and hard-working Early Reader Team read this book prior to publication and provided their comments, critiques, and corrections: *Susan Beatty, Stephanie Brancati, Kathy Collins, David Congdon, Brenda Dahlfors, Beth Dancy, Loranda Daniels Buoy, Nancy Diestler, Lynda Fergus, Pat Gerber, Lt. Edward Gritzner, Sgt. Jason Hall, Lynn Hirshman, Michelle Love, Steven Maresso, Lisa McCann, Elaine Montgomery, T/C Rita Moore, Rebecca Paciorek, Linda Pautz, Sam Petitto (ret. police officer), Sanda Putnam, JoAnn Schutte, Kathy Skorstad, Judy Tucker, Kimberly Wade, Carol D. Westover,* and *Mary-Jane Woodward.* Many thanks for your sharp eyes!

Thanks to *Matt Mason Photography* (www.MattMasonPhotography.com) for the photo of the Mailboat that became the front cover, *W. J. Goes* for escorting my photography crew around the lake in his Boston whaler, and *Maryna Zhukova* of MaryDes (www.MaryDes.eu) for the cover design. Maryna, I'm happy this one was your favorite. All your covers are my favorite.

Rebecca Paciorek, Susan Beatty, and *JoAnn Schwartz Schutte* of Blue Dot Marketing (http://rpaciorek8.wixsite.com/bluedotdigitalmkt), you are the best promotions team an author could ask for.

A big thanks to *my readers* for supporting my writing habit. When I put up the pre-order for this book—with no cover art and no book description—you stepped right up and asked for your copies. Thank you for believing in me that much. I am grateful and deeply respect the fact that you trust your leisure hours to me.

Finally, thanks to *Fergus* my black cat for hogging half the pillow every night (and purring in my ear). Thanks to my German Shepherd *Angel* for finally outgrowing the puppy phase. Actually, I love you. You are such a good girl. And thanks to my boyfriend *Charles William Maclay* for holding me up when I'm tired, holding my hand on our walks, and holding my heart for always.

ABOUT THE AUTHOR

Danielle Lincoln Hanna is the author of the Mailboat Suspense Series. While she now lives in the Rocky Mountains of Montana, her first love is still the Great Plains of North Dakota where she was born. When she's not writing, you can find her hiking with her boyfriend Charles, adventuring with her German Shepherd Angel, and avoiding surprise attacks from her cat Fergus.